T0165487

THE
TEMPTATION
TRIANGLE

One Woman's Journey Through Each Side of an Extramarital Affair,
the Lust, the Lovers and the LIES...

Based on a True Story

MICHELLE SCALES

Order this book online at www.trafford.com
or email orders@trafford.com

Most Trafford titles are also available at major online book retailers.

© Copyright 2011 Michelle Scales.
All rights reserved. No part of this publication may be reproduced, stored in a retrieval
system, or transmitted, in any form or by any means, electronic, mechanical, photocopying,
recording, or otherwise, without the written prior permission of the author.

Printed in the United States of America.

Thanks to: Editor Leah Steele. Dear Friends and
Collaborators - Suzie Parker-Jones & Susan Rennie.
Book Cover design and internal formatting; Michelle Scales, Designing M Style, Australia

ISBN: 978-1-4269-9322-0 (sc)
ISBN: 978-1-4269-9323-7 (e)

Trafford rev. 08/27/2011

 www.trafford.com

North America & international
toll-free: 1 888 232 4444 (USA & Canada)
phone: 250 383 6864 ♦ fax: 812 355 4082

For you who are wondering
what it would be like;
to be tempted,
to be cheated on,
to tempt others,
and to (possibly) get caught!

For those needing help to withstand;
A cheating partner,
A promise from a married man,
or your cheating self,
know there is light at the end of the tunnel,
and know you can fulfil your dreams.

Dedicated to my loving husband, who puts up with all of me and more.
For his understanding and his knowledge that I will be true to him,
til death, we do part... (or will I ?)

In memory of the relationships that went before,
that sculpted and created the woman I am today and taught me
how to enjoy the act of sex and the flirtatious Me!

Thanks to Dan, Nick and Harry for allowing me to share our
stories so that it may help others.

THE
TEMPTATION
TRIANGLE

A triangle has three sides.
No matter how you turn it around,
there are still three sides.
Sometimes the sides are equal.
Sometimes they are not.

In a marriage, there are also three sides.
A wife, her husband and temptation!
Sometimes these sides are equal.
Sometimes they are not.

Written by Michelle (Shelly) Leigh Scales

About the Author

I was born and raised in Sydney Australia, by my beautiful, loving parents.

Being the sister in the middle of two brothers we enjoyed a great Aussie sun-drenched beach life.

I witnessed first hand the joy of parents who remained married for their entire adult lives and I grew up expecting nothing less for my life also.

From the early age of fourteen I started writing daily in a small 'locked' diary. I captured my life's daily events and shared my feelings openly with the blank pages of my tiny books. I mostly wrote about boys back then. I would keep a list in the back of all the spunky boys and would collect movie tickets, cards and letters and paste them onto the pages. I still continue my diary today, however the entries are a little more sophisticated, more of a gratitude journal with (thankfully) fewer 'boys' listed in the back!

Unfortunately, or fortunately, my life did take a very different path from that of my parents. From heart breaks and tears, to the excitement and thrill of new love. I hope my story will touch you in many ways.

My most treasured times are those of big belly laughs with my friends and family.

Cheers

Michelle

I want to share with you my experience from each side of The Temptation Triangle;

A wife, whose husband cheated with another woman,

The other woman, who cheated with someone else's husband,

And a wife, who cheated on her husband with another man...

The world is full of wonderful people and wonderful relationships.

It's not a matter of how many relationships you have but about how you treat your relationships and those in it. Also important is what you learn from your relationships, what you choose to leave behind and what you choose to take with you to your next relationship.

I don't profess to be an expert on this subject but I have lived a fascinating life when it comes to relationships.

I hope you enjoy my journey through the three sides of The Temptation Triangle. It was fun to go back and revisit old haunting memories and to learn from my many treasured diary entries.

Remember, there is power in a diary...

there is power in writing...

There is power in YOU!

CONTENTS

TRIANGLE SIDE 1

"So Dan told you then?"

"Cory, what are you talking about?"

From the tone in Cory's voice it was obvious. Cory claimed, to know nothing... 'You're not getting away with it that easy', I thought.

I asked him straight out - "Is Dan having an affair?"

"Talk to Dan" he says.

"Is it Kristina?" I ask.

No answer - well that obviously means 'yes'. So next question is "For how long?" No answer, equals - it must be a while!

How could Dan say to Cory that he was going to tell me and then for me to find out like this. Cory felt awful.

I couldn't believe it. I was angry! I was angry at Dan, I was angry at Kristina and I was even more angry at myself.

I was 24 years old. It was 1993.

I was a young woman who left school and spent a year at Williams Secretarial School before entering the work force. I started my career as a Junior Receptionist. I enjoyed being the face of the office. Meeting and introducing people as they came in contact with our company.

My first job was in a solicitor's office. In 1989 I changed jobs to a large computer software company based in Epping. Travelling to Epping from Collaroy Plateau was no fun at all, sitting in traffic every morning, it was so frustrating and boring. I knew the company was due to relocate to Neutral Bay in four months, so I had to hang in there.

The people were great and the opportunity to move up the corporate ladder within the company was a strong incentive, not to mention the extra money.

Six weeks after I joined, Dan started work on the I.T. Help Desk. Dan had a lovely smile and I enjoyed his camaraderie every time he walked past my desk.

In August we packed up the offices and relocated to new premises at Neutral Bay.

Knowing I was single, Dan was always trying to match me up with Ryan. Ryan was a nice guy but not quite what I wanted in my man! Ryan was secretly dating another work colleague so he wasn't interested in me. I was enjoying a bit of a phone fling with Mitch from our Melbourne office. A very tall (6'7") long lanky dude with a wicked sense of humour. Mitch found many reasons to call the Sydney office and have long chats. Pity he was such a long way away...

After-work drinks on a Friday became a regular event. Sitting on the balcony overlooking the Harbour Bridge and the city lights was a great way to end the working week. Sometimes Dan and I would talk for ages with another new team member 'BIG' Dan. Big Dan was a sweetie and yes, we needed to call him Big Dan because he was a large cuddly man. Dan and Big Dan had worked together previously, so they had spent loads of time together and were the best of friends. I was now part of their clique. Dan, Big Dan and me.

We would lunch together often at the restaurants around Neutral Bay. My favourite was The Oaks Hotel as it was always cheery and relaxing. Big Dan always wanted to go to the local Indian Restaurant across the road. He enjoyed hot spicy lunches to the point of needing extra napkins to wipe away the sweat that dripped from his forehead from the extra hot chillies.

Big Dan loved it when Dan brought in leftovers from his parent's place. They would have big weekend Fijian Indian cook ups. This was Big Dan's favourite, home cooked curry and chilli dishes.

Dan didn't live with his parents, he was living in Parramatta with an old work colleague Tina, they had been sharing a unit for almost a year.

My relationship with Dan was developing into something deeper than a friendship. He was a real charmer. Very polite, sweet and easy to talk to. My interest in him was increasing daily.

Diary Entry:

Friday October 6th

Was a busy day getting ready for our Managing Director's Farewell Party. Dan and I sat out on the balcony all by ourselves and he kissed me very passionately. WOW it was such a sexy kiss. Afterwards we went parking at Blue's Point Reserve and had a wonderful night together. He's thinking of coming with me to USA and Canada. Oh he's so nice – I'm falling in love, very much so. He said that he is in love but not sure just how much. I rang Big Dan to share the news. Oh!!!! Can't sleep.

So that's how it all started, we were great friends and then after one very long suggestive kiss on the balcony and a few hours (four to be exact) at Blue's Point with many more seductive kisses, our love grew. Everyone loved him, especially my mum. I think she loved his dark skin and his beautiful smile more than I did. He was extremely polite and always well mannered. The perfect gentleman! My perfect gentleman!

At the time of our first kiss, Dan was living with Tina and according to Dan, Tina was just a 'friend'. Apparently their living arrangements hadn't been great for the last six months. After five weeks of being 'with' me, he decided to move back home with his family. I helped him move his stuff and met Tina in the process. She was a nice lady.

We spent a lot of our spare time with Dan's family. He had a very large Fijian Indian family, with lots of aunts, uncles and cousins. We would have picnics and BBQ's in the Royal National Park near their Cronulla home.

Dan had great friends too. There was Jono, Cory and Simon. They had been friends since high school and they played competition basketball every Tuesday night. We always had so much fun with the 'guys' and their wives. Jono was married to Georgina and Simon was married to Laura. Cory and Dan were the last of the gang to tie the knot. Jono and Simon always teased them about 'who was going to be next'.

We also hung out at Big Dan's place at Glenmore Park (near Penrith). Big Dan was married to Miss Lynnie and they had two small boys.

The three of us, Big Dan, Dan and I would hide away in the back shed and listen to Dire Straits while they would talk their computer talk amongst themselves.

Diary Entry:

Sunday March 18th

We had so much fun today at Cronulla Beach. Dan and his cousins played cricket and us girls chatted away. Dan decided to throw me in the water. It was a lot of fun. We all got burnt (more sunscreen next time). I enjoy spending time with Dan and his family.

Our time together was precious as we lived over an hour apart from each other. We would spend every lunch together at work and as much time after work as possible. I slept many nights at Dan's parent's place. It was easier to stay over than drive home to my folks late at night. Plus I got to sleep next to my new boyfriend.

Diary Entry:

Thursday June 21st

Oh I'm so excited. Tomorrow I'm on my way to Hawaii. Three days in Honolulu then on to Vancouver and travel across half of Canada. I can't wait to get in the air and on to my adventure. I know I will miss Dan. He has become close to me over the last months.

June and July saw me leave Australia for a trip to Canada. I had relatives there and I wanted to enjoy travelling before settling down. Before flying out Dan and I cooled off our relationship. Going away for eight weeks was a 'long time'.

On my return, I realised I was missed. Dan smothered me with love and affection. He was so excited to have me back home. I was feeling great about myself. I had just travelled on my own for two months and was on top of the world. I felt I was ready for any challenge. The weekend after I got back we took a day trip to the Woronora Dam, had a romantic picnic and took cute photos of each other. It was good to be home. It was good to be with Dan again. Our relationship just picked up where it left off.

My friendship with Big Dan continued to grow too. We spent time together whenever we could. Big Dan always talked about the two of us going freesia picking in Spring. He tried to convince me that the scent of the wild freesias were so much stronger. I thought he was overdoing it a bit! Until...

Diary Entry:

Saturday September 15th

Oh my - we have so many flowers, I don't know what we are going to do with them all. Both Big Dan and I each got a bucket full of freesias. We went freesia picking along the roads to Palm Beach. They are just so gorgeous. I hope they last for a while. I plan to dry some tomorrow. Mum is loving having them - the perfume is amazing. Thanks Big Dan for a memory I will treasure forever.

Yes Big Dan took me Freesia picking. I love this memory. It was a great trip up along the Northern Beaches in Big Dan's blue Suzuki Sierra. We had our big buckets in the back of the car ready for a load or two of flowers. Newport was our first stop. We found wild freesias growing along the side of the road. I had never even noticed them before. Big Dan was right, it was fun and the scent filled the car. It was so strong we had to wind down the windows to breathe. It was a wonderful (and most memorable) night. We had lots of laughs and we talked about my future with Dan.

Shortly afterwards, I received a promotion to Sales Assistant. I trained up the new receptionist and started my new role in a sales team of five sales people.

Diary Entry:

Friday September 28th

Big Dan kissed me... yes he did. And not just a peck on the cheek. He wants to be with me... I'm with Dan. Oh my... I told him I can't be with him. He has a wife and two little kids. What was he thinking. I feel bad for him now. Did I lead him on? We were just friends... weren't we?

The night was dark and stormy... no it wasn't. I've just always wanted to write that. The night was a fun one out with our work friends. We dropped Dan off at North Sydney Station and then I drove to the Artarmon Motor Inn where Big Dan's car was parked and we sat and talked for ages.

Big Dan started to share how he was feeling towards me. I was totally shocked. I didn't realise how much he loved me. He leaned over and kissed me... it was all engulfing. I was overwhelmed. I couldn't kiss him back... it wasn't right! I told him that we couldn't be and that was the last time it was discussed. Our friendship never suffered for it but I always felt a bit guarded around him.

Big Dan was like a father figure to me. Someone I could discuss anything with. He wrote many beautiful poems and letters for me. I have shared some of these treasured writings in this book.

Author's Learning:
This was my first 'Temptation Triangle' experience and I didn't even realise it at the time. It certainly can creep up on you - so be careful.

Diary Entry:

Friday October 3rd

Today I got my invitation to Deana's wedding. I'm so excited to be part of this wonderful family. Deana's Husband-to-be has asked Dan to be the best man... I guess it will be all wedding talk from now on. Hope that doesn't mean pressure for us.

I was invited to Dan's sister's wedding. Deana was younger than Dan, so for her to be getting married before her big brother was a bit unusual for their traditional family. First born were always the first to get married. There was a lot of pressure for Dan to pop the question to me... and quickly! I was feeling special being welcomed into his family this way. Everyone was so nice and it was wonderful experiencing this different culture.

Diary Entry:

Saturday November 3rd

Today at Dan's I found an old ring of Tina's. I can't believe I didn't realise that they were 'more than friends'... Oh well – her loss. My gain! I'm glad he chose me... a little bit annoyed that he didn't tell me the truth!

I found a ring in Dan's bed-side table which he had engraved for Tina. It was kind of plain with an embossed flower pattern all the way around it. I asked him why he had it. They obviously were more than 'friends'. He announced, "You can have it if you want," to which I replied "No thanks, I want my own".

Not long after that, Dan did buy me my own ring, more like a wedding band than an engagement ring. He said it was our friendship ring. 'Okay, we'll go with that', I thought at the time. I was a little bit disappointed, okay a lot disappointed that it didn't contain a diamond and a proposal.

Our families thought the ring was more significant and the next thing I knew it was all on - WE WERE GETTING MARRIED! There was no real proposal, no one knee on the ground or anything... no big fat diamond - - - what happened to *my* perfect gentleman?

Author's Learning:
It's amazing when you are in the moment, you don't take a step back and look at the big picture. Being the centre of everyone's attention can be exciting and the thought of a wedding can be alluring.
The first lie was cast - learning that Tina was more than a friend should have set off the alarm bells ringing in my head. I should have listened to that inner voice speaking and saying - "Warning, Warning... what are you doing? Wait for the diamond!!!"

A few weeks later, Greg (a fellow colleague) offered me an opportunity to house-sit his home at Penshurst while he was transferred overseas for 12 months. I was going to be living just down the road from Dan. It was perfect, now we could be closer. Dan spent many nights sleeping over at my new pad.

Christmas morning we drove over an hour to my folks and celebrated Christmas lunch with my family. Then off to Dan's family for dinner. It felt like we spent the entire day on the road travelling. I was exhausted, not to mention how much I over-ate.

Diary Entry:

Monday January 7th

I returned to work today after a great Christmas/New Year break. Others were called back from their extended holidays to receive the news that the company was downsizing and we were being made redundant. I was the last one on the list. We all went out to lunch. I felt sorry for those who had to go back to the office, because they would now have to do their jobs and ours. Tomorrow... Dan and I are looking for work.

Dan and I were both retrenched just after Christmas break. I found a new secretarial job in Surry Hills. Dan started working on a programming job with Big Dan.

Many months passed, we continued our lives in our 'borrowed' pad in Penshurst. Dan was sleeping over more and more, however he had not 'officially' moved in. It was a great time in our lives I was enjoying my new job with a franchise company and Dan was earning okay money working from home.

Dan bought me a kitten from our local pet shop we named her Kayla. She was a chocolate Persian and was totally adorable except she used to poop on the lounge room carpet rug every morning. Not a nice thing to wake up to every day. We never got her to use the litter tray but we did teach her to walk on the lead. People thought it was funny 'walking a cat!'

Diary Entry:

Friday Apri 12th

Wow Deana's wedding was beautiful. She looked so pretty. They had a beautiful day followed by a fun party. We didn't get home til 2am. Dan looked so handsome as the best man. A man in a suit always makes me weak at the knees.

It was fun being part of the preparations for Deana's wedding. I felt very privileged to share her big day. I know she will do the same for me when it's my turn. The flowers and the dresses were gorgeous. Her bridesmaids wore soft musk pink and the flowers were all white. Dan looked pretty hot in his tuxedo. Guys should be required to look that good everyday...

Our wedding plans were coming along nicely.

My dress was borrowed from a family friend and we were going to have a lovely garden wedding in the Sydney Royal Botanical Gardens. The plan was for me to arrive at the top of the eighty steps near Mrs Macquarie's Chair and make my descent into my new life to marry my husband.

I hand-made and hand-painted all the invitations. They were sent out and everything was set. Then five weeks before the big day Dad decided I really should have a new dress, a wedding dress of my own. So off to the shops we went. The one we found was beautiful but it was three sizes too big and needed some major adjusting which involved weekly trips back to the store for fittings.

Our new life together was all on track.

Diary Entry:

Saturday October 19th

Today we found our new home. After a day in the car looking at horrible apartments, we fell madly in love with a Semi in RABY !!! I know, not where I wanted to live either but it's such a great little place. I love it. Can't wait to move all our stuff in... YIPPEE !!! Our new home, our life together. It's going to be so great.

We bought a house in Raby (near Campbelltown). Driving around with the real estate agent, I specifically asked him not to show me anywhere in Raby because I couldn't imagine living in a place with such an unfortunate name. And then we saw this beautiful, brand new semi that still had the builder's rubbish out the front and I knew we had to have it. When the real estate agent told me we were in Raby - I didn't care. This was my home. It was new and fresh and just what we wanted.

We moved most of our furniture (what little we had) prior to the wedding. We didn't live there before we got married - that wasn't the right thing to do. It was going to be nice and new for us as a married couple. We'd get home from the honeymoon to start our new lives together.

Diary Entry:

Friday November 8th

Big Day nearly here. This time next week I will be getting excited and a bit nervous. Last fitting tomorrow. Can't wait to see my special dress all finished. Still deciding what to do with my hair... up

... down ... not sure. Have tried the hairdressers but not happy with their results. Have decided to do it myself – after all it is my hair. Have to confirm numbers tomorrow... we have 84 people coming. It's going to be fun.

Finally we were all organised. We just had to wait for the big day to arrive. Everything was as ready as it could be. Flowers - check; dress - check; shoes - check; venue - check; rings - check; groom - check....

Diary Entry:

Thursday November 14th

Well it's happened. I have now had 'sex'. After dinner out, Dan and I left early and returned home to his parents place, on the floor in the living room. Wow... it wasn't as exciting as I thought it was going to be. Oh well... I love him for trying to make it special. I know Saturday night will be better, now that my first time is officially over.

So, I lost my virginity just days before our wedding. We had been out to dinner with Dan's extended family and we left early to get home before everyone else. Dan obviously had plans that I wasn't aware of.

We 'made love' (that's what we called it back then) on the living room floor of Dan's parent's house. Not the most romantic situation I could have imagined. We were sleeping in the living room because there were so many family members in town for our wedding. We couldn't sleep in Dan's room, as that was occupied by Uncle Jed and his wife Rosie from Canberra.

I don't remember very much of my first experience. Lying under Dan and knowing that this was my first time was not memorable at all. Being a good Christian girl with a good moral upbringing I knew it was the 'right' thing to do, to wait for 'Mr Right' to come along. Things could only pick up for me in the 'love making' department.

My parents brought me up to know right from wrong. We went to church meetings three times a week. The meetings taught me that prayer and reading the bible were important, being good unto others, etc. etc. However, sex and the activities within a marriage were never discussed. So I was going into this marriage BLIND! Yes I knew what sex was but I didn't know enough. I was naive - very very naive!

Dan attended our church meetings with me for a few months when we first got engaged but decided that they were not for him. Being brought up in a Catholic home, he had chosen to be non-practicing Catholic.

Diary Entry:

Saturday November 16th – My Wedding Day

What a day... I'm wishing I had an earlier Wedding time... the day went on forever. It was a beautiful day – apart from the RAIN. At least there was no one in the Gardens when we had our photos taken. I know they are going to turn out just beautiful. Tonight we are in North Sydney, so this is the start of my new life. A married woman. Who would believe it... Me, Mrs Shandra....

It seems weird in a way. Can't wait until tomorrow – we are off on our honeymoon and I don't know where we are going. I hate surprises... I don't need a passport, so it's somewhere in Australia. I'm praying for good weather! We consummated our marriage, although it was just a formality really. Too tired to see any stars!!!

It had been raining since 5am and was still raining at 5pm. I had been ready for over an hour (in typical me fashion). As we waited for the clock to tick by to our departure time, dad put his hand on my shoulder and said, "You don't have to do this you know?" I just stared at him. Why would he say that? I couldn't answer. It seemed like such a weird thing to say at this time. Could we postpone it for a week and hope for better weather? Or was he talking about forever? Not a good time to think about an answer. We continued waiting.

It was finally time to leave. We drove across the Roseville Bridge, the rain was so heavy on the windscreen, the wipers were working at extra speed. Dad was sitting with me in the back seat holding my hand so tight that it felt like my blood had stopped flowing. 'Is the rain ever going to stop?' I thought.

Lee turned and leaned over from the front seat, she was my bridesmaid and she knew how I was feeling about the rain. I could see *my* disappointment reflected in her eyes.

As we crossed the famous Sydney Harbour Bridge, the sun came out, the rain stopped and it was stunning. I quickly called the venue from the car's mobile and said, "Lets have the wedding in the gardens, please move all the people." "Too late" came the reply - everyone is here, ready and waiting. My heart sank, my dream of a garden wedding was gone!

The wedding was lovely, we exchanged our vows on the veranda of The Restaurant on the Park where we also had the reception.

We had beautiful photos taken at the Art Gallery and in the Royal Botanical Gardens. There were no people around due to the entire day of rain. The evening went so fast. I don't remember eating. I know I did some dancing because we have photos of that. But before I knew it I was back in the wedding car waving goodbye and being taken to our hotel. We were both tired, drained and there was no thought of any 'special' love making that night.

I was anxious to know where I was going for our honeymoon, as that had been up to Dan to organise everything and surprise me.

Dan took me to Noosa for our honeymoon. I remember boarding a plane to Maroochydore and thinking - where the hell is that? Not knowing it was just down the road from one of the most spectacular places in Australia.

Diary Entry:

Monday November 18th

Our apartment is nice. Tiled floors in every room. Big comfy bed and lounges. Dan is determined to have sex on the cold tiles, I told him he had to be on the bottom... We had a great day at the beach and home for 'love making' in the afternoon. Haven't experienced any *daytime sex... it's fun. Tomorrow we are up early and off to Fraser Island for the day to do some four wheel driving. Can't wait.*

Arriving at our honeymoon apartment we couldn't wait to explore this beautiful location. The weather was beautiful and there was so much to do and see. We booked a special four wheel drive tour to Fraser Island.

Fraser Island was beautiful. We travelled along the beach and saw wild dingos and rusty old ship wrecks. Lunch was amazing, a gorgeous seafood barbeque was awaiting us. We swam in the crystal clear water of Lake Mackenzie before heading back to Noosa.

We spent the rest of our days lounging by the pool and window shopping down Hastings Street.

It was relaxing spending time together. All we had to think about was where we would eat out each night.

We enjoyed sex regularly, just like most newly wed couples, I would imagine. Dan was very romantic when he wanted sex. I was learning fast - very fast.

Returning from our honeymoon, we settled into our new life and our new home. I attended a nearby church meeting in Bradbury and met some lovely friends. Tom and Sophie had lived in the area for over seven years and lived on a one acre property within walking distance from where we lived. It was nice to have an instant female friend that lived so close.

Sophie and I spent a lot of time together, especially on weekends when Dan was off playing golf. We would have 'Grannie' afternoon teas with home-made scones and lots of laughs. Tom and Sophie, Dan and I had games nights together and shared meals at each other's place.

I was commuting to the city everyday for my job. Dan was still working on developing accounting software, which we hoped would bring in the big dollars. It was extremely difficult living on my salary and the few hundred dollars Dan was getting.

Financially times were tough, we were only earning enough to pay the mortgage on our little home, which was more than my entire salary. There was only a small amount left each week to eat and to put petrol in our car to get to and from work. I remember needing warm clothes in winter and not having enough money to buy a $7.00 pair of tracky dacks from K-Mart.

It was also tough on our relationship. Not having money to spend on going out to dinner or to the movies made it stressful as well.

Ten months after we were married, Dan had a falling out with the other software partners, our big dream of financial freedom died. Dan needed to find another job fast!

Dan was offered a job with a large software company in Botany, just down the road from the Sydney airport. It was good to see him excited about being part of a large organisation again. We drove 90 minutes to the city every morning. Dropping Dan to work first, I would then go onto my work and then pick him up on my way home.

With more money coming in, our weekends were spent renovating the backyard. As we had moved into a newly built home, the backyard was dirt. We paved an entertaining area and planted ferns and shrubs.

Over the next months we bought another cat, a soft grey persian we named Gypsy. Shortly followed by a puppy we named Little Mike, because he was the runt of the litter. It was our little family; Kayla, Gypsy and Little Mike.

A year and a half passed quickly with not many diary entries to go through.

I could see that our relationship wasn't perfect. The sex wasn't as fantastic as I thought it would be. It wasn't what my expectations lead me to believe. I wasn't craving to be with Dan day and night. We would 'make love' often enough but there was certainly no sexual fantasies being fulfilled. My lack of interest and knowledge obviously wasn't helping.

I would often find Dan in the early hours of the morning, on the couch, fast asleep, still holding himself. I always felt weird about this but just accepted it was something guys did. My curiosity lead me to discover a secret stash of porn videos in our spare room. So that's what he did at night when I was asleep. No wonder he didn't have the desire to come to bed with me. I started to wonder how long this had been going on.

Diary Entry:

Wednesday August 8th

My period finally arrived today... only seven days late. I thought this was it... I thought I was going to be a mum to a little chocolate bub... oh well. we'll try again next month.

Dan and I had started to plan for children now that he had a good job and everything was getting better for us financially. I had stopped taking the pill. Maybe a beautiful baby would be the thing to make it special between us again.

Months of trying passed by.

Our relationship was still not great in the bedroom and I wasn't pregnant yet so I thought some counselling would be good for me and would hopefully benefit our marriage. I started seeing Jessica over in Randwick. Jessica was a psychologist specialising in relationships. I would meet with Jessica every week and she helped me work through many issues that I had about being raised in a religious family and what 'perceptions' and 'hang-ups' I had on intimacy. As the weeks passed, Jessica wanted Dan to join us for a session or two so she could help us together. He refused, he didn't think he needed help. "She can help you" he said, "I don't need a shrink!"

Dan was uncomfortable about me sharing our lives with Jessica. I knew it was helping me.

We made many memories sharing social times with Dan's work colleagues. On Friday afternoons I would meet them at the local pub near their offices and we would hang out for hours. They were a great bunch of people.

Dan received a promotion as National I.T. Manager. He was excited about climbing the corporate ladder. It was good seeing him happy. His colleagues were now his team. Nathan, chatted with me about how great it was that Dan was now his boss and how deserving he was of his new position.

Everything was looking up. I was getting help. Dan was enjoying his new role... until...

Dan's behaviour started to change shortly after receiving his promotion. Was it too much? Was the pressure getting to him? We would drive all the way to and from work and he became really quiet. He stopped telling me things. Simple things that were going on in the office, who he had lunch with and what the team were up to. I regularly asked what was wrong and the answer always came back 'Nothing!'

Author's Learning:
This was the first time I was aware of my 'gut' feeling (or intuition). I had heard about the concept before but now it was working hard and I should have listened and learnt from what it was trying to tell me.

We were playing snooker about a month later and I felt really uncomfortable being there. There was a woman all over my man, my husband. It was my first introduction to his newest team member, his 'secretary', Kristina. She flirted with Dan right in front of me. I shrugged it off at first thinking she was trying to fit in. After all - he was MY husband - full stop!

When I brought my discomfort to his attention and asked him to be careful, he acted like he didn't notice. His comment was, "don't be silly - it takes two to tango". I can still hear those words ringing in my ears. So, I accepted his faithfulness to me, his wife. He was aware of my feelings and I expected that should be enough for him to act responsibly.

For weeks I continued to share my concerns with Dan about Kristina's flirting, telling him that she could be trouble. Every time I saw her, I could see the determination in her eyes. She was in this for all she could get. She didn't care about me, our marriage or anything else that may have mattered.

Dan continued to be very blasé about the situation and just kept laughing it off. I was getting more annoyed every time I saw her.

And then arrived... **My Day of Grief.**

Diary Entry:

Saturday October 29th

I'm sad. I found out today that Dan and Kristina have been having an affair for a long time. I have cried so long that my eyes hurt. I'm tired. I can't talk about this now, maybe in a few days.

Saturday morning Dan took off first thing to play golf. A normal Saturday for us. But today was a bit different, after golf, the plan was for him to go and visit his sister Deana, who had just given birth to her first child and was still in the hospital. Then onto his parents (over an hour away). We were then meeting up that night at Jonathan and Georgina's to celebrate Jono's 30th birthday.

All seemed like a normal Saturday until... mid morning Cory (Dan's Best Man) called.

"Hi Michelle, how are *YOU?*" he asks.

"I'm fine" I reply.

"Wow, (pause) are you really?" Cory asks.

"Sure" says me, not knowing where this was going.

"So Dan told you then?" Cory questions.

"What?" Now I'm getting confused.

"Cory, what are you talking about?"

I can honestly say at this point I knew what was going on. Just from the tone in Cory's voice it was quite obvious.

Cory claimed to know nothing... 'You're not getting away with it that easy', I thought.

I straight out asked him, "Is Dan having an affair?"

"Talk to Dan" he says.

"Is it Kristina?" I ask.

No answer - well that obviously means yes to both of my questions.

So next question was "for how long?" ... No answer equalled - must be a while!

How could Dan say to Cory that he was going to tell me and then for me to find out like this. Cory felt awful.

I couldn't believe it. I was angry! I was angry at Dan, I was angry at Kristina and I was even more angry at myself.

Looking back, I knew what was going on. My intuition had been spot on. There was movement in my stomach. I just didn't listen to it. I didn't know *how* to listen to it. On my wedding day when Dad said "You don't have to do this..." he was right. He knew back then. Why didn't I?

So now it was time for me to take charge, 'man the battle stations!' ... and ATTACK!

My first call was to Dan's mobile. No answer...

My second call went to the golf club. I was put through to the club house. "Has Dan played golf today?" I asked, ready to pounce through the phone.

"No, sorry Ma'am, no Dan listed today."

I wanted to track him down. I wanted to scream and yell at him. I wanted to hit him! I wanted explanations! I wanted to cry!

My third call was to Nathan. Nathan was one of Dan's work mates that I had met at drinks. Nathan confirmed: "Sorry Michelle, Dan and Kristina have been together for months. They sneak out at lunch time and have sex in the car at the end of the (airport) runway."

"How do you know that?" I asked. "Because Dan tells us when he gets back". RIGHT! Nice of him to share this with his team!

So I'm feeling pretty rotten about now, to say the least.

Anger boils inside me.

Call number four went to Deana. Poor Deana, still in hospital, after giving birth to her first born son. Before even asking how she was, I demanded to know if she had seen Dan. "No, he hasn't been in to see me today," she replied.

"You sound upset Michelle, what's going on?"

"He's having an affair!" I just blurted it out. It came out so fast I couldn't catch it. It was the first time I had said it out loud. It was out now, there was no taking it back.

"WHAT?" she says. I go on to re-live the entire morning and what I have discovered. Poor Deana, her entire world changed in the blink of an eye. She just gave birth to a beautiful baby boy, she finds out her only brother has been cheating with his secretary and her favourite sister-in-law has been shattered. She handles it all really well and tries to comfort me but it's no use. We talk about it for a bit more and then it's on to call number five.

Call number five was to Dan's parents. It was his next planned stop after all. I can tell you at this point if I had any more information on Kristina, like her surname, address or phone number she would have been hearing from me. I would have let her have it. I wanted to blame someone and she was certainly an easy target.

Dan's father Bob answered the phone. "Hi Michelle . . . no, we haven't seen Dan, is everything okay?" Wrong question!

"Of course not, Dan's been having an affair with a girl from his work!" I announced.

Bob, now totally speechless, says "Hang on - I'll go get Mum". So Dan's mum Jackie picks up the second phone and I had both of them on the line.

Jackie, was angry, almost as angry as me. She had brought him up better! "Her son wouldn't do such a thing!" Jackie's solution was to get help!

"Father Vincent (their Catholic Priest) will be able to sit down and work this out with you both," concludes Jackie.

"WHO?" I'd never been to their church. What was their 'Father' going to do? I hadn't thought of working it out - I just wanted to hit Dan.

By now, I had shared my news with everyone that Dan was supposed to visit that day. It was time to confront him at Jono's birthday party. He would have to show up there. So I got myself together, had another cry and drove 55 minutes to get to Jono's place. Dan was not there yet. Jono and Simon, took one look at me and knew something wasn't right. I cried. I kept crying. In fact, I cried most of the night. Happy Birthday Jono! What a way to spoil his 30th birthday party.

Jono, Simon and their wives Georgina and Laura were very supportive.

Jono and Georgina had been through a similar affair situation in the previous year. Jonathan had cheated on Georgina with another woman. Georgina had agreed to take him back on the promise he would never do it again. Georgina had two children with Jono and didn't want her children to grow up without their father around full time. So us girls made a pact right then and there, to tell each other if we ever found out that our husbands were cheating.

Georgina and Laura hadn't known about Kristina. But the guys sure DID! They knew it had been going on for a long time. UN-be-liev-able...

Dan never arrived at the party. Where was he? How could he not show? Jonathan was one of his best mates. A mate that we had shared Christmas holidays with. A mate whose children's christenings we had attended.

I drove home alone as the tears rolled down my face. I was totally exhausted.

After a nice hot shower, I crawled into bed. About half an hour later, Dan arrived home.

He said 'Hi', then jumped in the shower like nothing had happened. I wanted to yell out, "Hello! Where were you tonight???" but I said nothing.

I laid there for a while deciding what I would say. 'Stay calm,' I told myself. Try and get all the answers before you get angry.

After his long shower, he attempted to get into bed along side me. I stopped him.

"What do you think you're doing?" I asked.

"What are you talking about?" he said.

"Where were you tonight? How come you didn't come to Jono's Party?"

I wanted answers and I wanted them now! I was in no mood to wait.

"I was just with some friends" he said.

"FRIENDS???" I questioned. "Or just ONE friend?"

At this point he knew that I knew. He sat on the edge of the bed, hung his head and said, "I wanted to tell you but I just didn't know how."

"So you let Cory tell me?" "How could you?" I questioned.

I was so exhausted I didn't have the energy to fight or argue.

Loads of words came out that night. Loads of words that meant nothing anymore. What I remember most was holding myself together and being extremely strong. Being the woman that was too good for him.

I remember his words - that he loved me, that I was his 'best friend'. But she was his 'soul-mate'! ...and that he wanted to keep us both! *What planet did he think we were living on!*

After all the talking, he thought I was okay. He proceeded to get into MY bed again. NO SIR !!!

"Go sleep on the couch and tomorrow you can pack your things and leave." I was so angry and so tired.

I picked up my diary, my old faithful friend and made my entry.

The next morning he left. No sorry, nothing. He just left. He took a small sports bag full of clothes and went to his mum's. She wouldn't let him stay there. She was angry too and disowned him.

So where do you think he ended up. That's right - Kristina's place, with her parents.

The next few days were sad. My body ached in pain. Regular telephone calls with Dan were full of fighting and bitterness. There was no thought, on my part, of trying to fix this. There was no point, he had made his decision clear. He wasn't coming back.

The nights were the hardest, alone in the house with our pets. I cried until it felt like I had run out of tears. I realised we had issues but I never thought it would end like this. At the time it all seemed so sudden.

My dad called a 'family meeting' to share my news with the family! It was awkward to speak with them but at the same time it was good to get it off my chest. There was no real discussion, more like a statement. I felt like the biggest failure. My marriage was over. I had failed my marriage.

Author's Learning:
This was the perfect time for me to get help. Looking back I should have gone back to visiting with Jessica. I tried to handle all these feelings and frustrations on my own. That didn't work. Keeping everything bottled up inside was extremely toxic.

Diary Entry:

Monday November 16th

Today was our 2nd Wedding Anniversary... I feel really sad. I'm still here, I hate being all alone in this house. It certainly doesn't feel like my home anymore. I have started packing up my things. Dan didn't contact me today - not surprised.

Our second wedding anniversary came and went.

Diary Entry:

Sunday November 22nd

I am coming to terms with my new life. I have put the house on the market and continued packing ready to move back in with Mum and Dad. It's sad and lonely being in the house by myself. Glad to have my pets. I just want this to be over and to be happy again.

After packing up the house, I set off to my parents for some TLC. God knows I really needed some. I had been wounded, beaten down and trodden on. . . so the saying goes. Mum and Dad were very angry. Their little girl had been hurt so plans were made for me to come home and live with them.

The agreement between Dan and I was that we would sell our house and I would profit 100% of any of the monies made. Excellent plan - or so I thought. I ended up paying money in legal fees to sell the house.

I lived in the house until it was sold and contracts were exchanged. Everything was shipped back to Mum's, pets included. That's right - everything. I took the lot. I was an injured woman seeking some sort of compensation and revenge.

Actually , not everything. I left his clothes. I left his golf clubs, the TV and stereo, which he brought into the relationship and his collection of porn videos, of course.

Dan didn't come to collect his things, he sent his family instead. It was awkward when his Mum, Dad and sister arrived to get his stuff, they were quite surprised by his little 'collection'.

Diary Entry:

Tuesday November 24th

I followed Kristina and Dan home to her house. I felt like spitting on her but I didn't. I just offered Dan to her on a silver platter. I then walked away and cried. It's over. My marriage is over.

A few days later, I followed Dan and Kristina home from work to Kristina's parent's place. I was going to confront her. I wanted to let her know what she had done to me. That she had ruined my marriage, that she had taken away my man. That I was hurt and she was to blame.

I sat outside for a long time before I found the courage to walk to the front door. After knocking, Kristina's father came to the door. He was a very large man. I froze. I asked to see Kristina. As Kristina came to the door, my mood instantly changed, I just stood there and boldly told her "Good luck - you can have him!" Dan soon appeared behind her... surprise, surprise... and I said nothing further, I shook my head, turned and walked away.

I drove home, crying most of the way. Kristina wasn't the only one to blame. I was so disappointed in myself for what had happened to my marriage. I had failed. Why didn't he love me anymore? Why was she better than me? Why didn't I see this coming? Why did I react so differently? Why didn't I spit on her? Why did I put myself through that? Too many questions and I was too exhausted to care. All three of us were to blame for the part we played in this triangle.

I pulled into our driveway and the sight of the for sale sign with it's big "SOLD" sticker on it made me cry even more. It was like the end had finally arrived. The final curtain had fallen, it was real - it was over!

I immediately put the car in reverse and backed out of the driveway and proceeded to Sophie's place for a shoulder to cry on. Tom answered the door. He took one look at me and thought I had been beaten. I had mascara running down my face and my eyes were red and puffy. Tom instantly went into defence mode, ready to fight. "NO NO" I said, Dan didn't hit me. "Our house has sold!"

"What?" this was news to Tom and Sophie. They were my only friends that lived nearby and I hadn't told them anything. All they knew was there was this sad girl on their door step, in tears and they did not know why.

Sophie was a trooper. With her new baby in one arm and me under the other, we went upstairs for a good old heart to heart. She couldn't believe I had been going through all this stuff and I hadn't told her.

That was just the way I was brought up. 'You kept things to yourself. You didn't go airing your dirty laundry around. You don't need to get help, just get on with it - you'll be right!'

Two years of marriage over, just like that.

In the following months after selling the house, Dan and I continued to fight over many things that he believed he should have got, like our clothes dryer and washing machine. His thinking was because his Aunty and Uncle bought something for our wedding present, then he should have it. He wasn't happy when I told him I had sold the washing machine for $5.00 to a friend of mine. I hadn't really - it was my new 'don't mess with me' attitude. He wasn't getting anything.

I kept a list in the back of my diary as to who got the 'stuff'; Brother - Fridge, Susan - Washing Machine, Joanne - Dryer. Really it all just ended up in Dad's garage along with all our other possessions.

The road ahead was difficult and challenging for a long time. Music and the words found in sad country love songs helped me get through my sad times. It was good to be home with Mum and Dad and to have their support. It was also good to have some time alone.

I changed jobs soon after the New Year. I found a great job with a beauty company closer to home. The change was good. Having to show up for work everyday with no one knowing what I had just been through was my life saver. Work kept me busy and gave me something other than me to focus on.

Dan and I spoke less and less as the months and years passed.

Moral of Side I:

Being the one to get hurt, really hurts. It aches through to the core of your being. You question yourself, why why why and why? Why did this happen to me? What could I have done differently?

We all have relationship patterns. Dan's pattern was to overlap from one girlfriend to another. He had always had a girl on his arm ever since he was sixteen years old. This was a sign, a very BOLD sign. A sign I didn't see at the time. Patterns are something to look for.

Sex is to be enjoyed by both parties, not just one. If one person is not getting enough, or not enjoying it with the one they are with - they may be tempted elsewhere. Understand your partner's needs and expectations and do all you can to make them happy, as they should do for you too.

The best thing you can do if there are issues in your relationship is to communicate. If you don't speak up, how will your partner know there are any issues? And, more importantly what those issues are.

Dr Phil says, "Remember that people who have nothing to hide, hide nothing. Look for the common sense warning signs: A shift in patterns, accessibility, money, reliability and secrecy. A sudden great interest in grooming or dress, going to the gym, or putting on cologne. Also, remember not to accuse your partner because of unhealthy jealousy, which could hurt the trust between you."

What happened next:

Dan and I divorced and I worked through my sadness. My new job offered me the opportunity to meet new people . . . a fresh beginning, new relationships - no more missionary position for me!

I discontinued with church meetings. Looking back now I can see that Dan was my "out". Subconsciously I knew if I was with Dan and he didn't want to be part of the church then I didn't need to be part of it either. Making the decision to be 'with him' was an easy, gutless decision for me.

Big Dan remained married to his lovely wife and their two boys grew into fine young men. We are still in contact today.

Over the next five years Dan and Kristina had three boys. Kristina left Dan for another man and took their children with her. Dan gets to see his children every other weekend. How's that for karma? Dan has had other wives since!

It was now my turn to rebel. To do something a (tiny) bit naughty ... read on to Triangle Side 2.

TRIAD

You want to know
How it will be
You and him
or you and me
You just stand there
Your long hair blowing
Eyes alive your mind still growing
Saying to me
What can we do now that we both love you
I love you too
I don't really see
Why can't we go on as three

You are afraid
Embarrassed too
No one has ever said
Such a thing to you
Your mother's ghost
Stands on your shoulder
Face like ice a little bit colder
Saying to you
You can not do that
It breaks all the rules, you learnt in school
I don't really see
Why can't we go on as three

We love each other
It's plain to see
There's just one answer
That comes to me
Sister lovers
Water brothers
And in time maybe others
So you see
What we can do
Is try something new, if you're crazy to
I don't really see
Why can't we go on as three

Song : Jefferson Airplane

TRIANGLE SIDE 2

Today he is back in town! He has just arrived in the office. We can't wait. We meet in our secret stairwell. We try to control ourselves. It's not easy. I have been waiting for weeks to see him. It's so good to have him back again.

After work I race to the hotel. I arrive, park in the underground car park, watch to make sure I don't recognise anyone or they don't recognise me. I sneak through the back entrance up to room 329, hoping he's been upgraded to a nice hotel suite, not just a standard room. I have spent a lot of time in this hotel.

The door is ajar, he's expecting me. I dump my bags and stand with a huge smile on my face. Oh, how I have missed him.

I watch him lying in the bed, his long toned body, naked, on the crisp white hotel sheets, waiting for me to join him. I know this is going to be another great night. I'm sad he will be travelling home tomorrow to his wife. I will enjoy all of him now, while he is mine.

I was 29 years old. It was 1997.

Diary Entry:

Saturday December 16th

Last night was amazing! I met Nick from our Melbourne office. Can't believe how cute he is. I had such a great night with him, feeling a bit special. Oh and today is my birthday - very quiet day - Happy Birthday Me!

Leonie and I arrived at La Vino's Restaurant for our work Christmas party, the festivities were in full swing! Everyone had been drinking margaritas for a few hours when we arrived. There were extra people at the party from our Melbourne and Brisbane offices.

Nick Watkinson was there. Tall, dark, handsome with an athletic body that was totally to die for. But I wasn't the only one who had eyes for him. We exchanged eye contact throughout the party, they looked right through me as if he was trying to tell me that he wanted me then and there!

At one point, we found ourselves standing outside the restaurant, we both needed some air. We chatted for ages. He was really something.

Nick's voice was low, deep and sexy. The kind of voice that makes you weak at the knees when hearing it on the other end of the phone, but in person, it was even more enticing.

That night I was staying at Leonie's, we shared a cab ride home with Nick as he was staying at a hotel close to Leonie's place. Holding hands with Nick in the dark was fun... I had his right hand and I found out later Leonie was holding his left hand.

The FIGHT was on! No way was she having him. It was me he wanted. I was sure of that.

Leonie was our company's receptionist. She was a lovely lady with two young children. We had become great friends and enjoyed a party (or two). We were single and out to have a fun time.

I was now 29 and I had enjoyed other relationships since divorcing Dan. I felt I was much wiser and more capable of handling this type of relationship. Okay so he was married. I'd never been the 'other' woman before! I had no intention of being the 'other' woman for very long. He was going to be mine! All mine!

Now I know a bit about karma. Yes, I was aware that it might come back to bite me. Dan ended up being cheated on by Kristina with some other guy. And here I was finding myself falling crazy in love with a married man. What?? Why???

What was I thinking? I never wanted to be the 'other' woman. I certainly didn't want to hurt another woman the way I had been hurt.

These were just some of the questions that whirled in my mind.

Nick was nice, really nice but he belonged to someone else. I kept saying to myself, "Come on, haven't you learnt anything from your relationship with Dan?"

So what happened next? Well we flirted a little on the phone, then a little more and then, before we knew it there was absolutely no turning back.

Diary Entry:

Monday December 18th

Nick called early tonight. Two hours on the phone – he's in Adelaide for work.

This was the point where reality set in. I realised this was not going to be a normal relationship. There were going to be secrets, many, many secrets. There was going to be a lot of hiding and lying. I was not happy about that but I just wanted him for myself.

Diary Entry:

Wednesday December 20th

Another busy day. Nick called 3 times and we spoke forever – "WHAT am I doing?"

I loved talking to him. He was so easy to talk to. I knew I should stop this before it got out of control but I felt it was too late for that. My feelings were deep for him already.

I spent Christmas with my folks, pondering what I had got myself involved in. It was a weird feeling being in this situation, not being in control. I never thought I would find myself on this side of The Temptation Triangle. But it happened. I had to admit I wanted it to happen with Nick! It was exciting, it was new and it was WRONG!

All my childhood, I followed all the rules, learnt right from wrong. I learnt what was proper and what wasn't. How society expected you to behave. That you didn't sleep around. That you weren't meant to have feelings for someone else's husband. These feelings certainly weren't proper! But how could I stop it? Did I want to? It was thrilling! It was naughty! It was wonderful!

I wanted to be bad. It was my time to be bad. I needed to be bad. I had been good for such a long time. I wanted to win him. He was my challenge. I was in this for the prize. I wanted him to choose me, to want me!

Author's Learning:
This can often be the reason why women go after married men. It's the thrill of the chase, it's the challenge that the man will choose them over their wives. It is all about the excitement of being the one who wins.

Nick was married to Rebecca, they had been together for five years. They lived in Brighton right on the water at Port Philip Bay in Melbourne. We always talked about his marriage, about how things hadn't been great for a long time. Of course, I was only getting his side of their story but why would I not believe him? He was honest, he was loving, trusting and very kind. They had started drifting apart some time ago because he travelled a lot and she had wanted him home to start a family.

A family, or lack of one was the main thing Nick and I had in common. We both didn't want children. I had wanted children when I was with Dan, cute chocolate brown ones. My desire to have children was now over.

Diary Entry:

Wednesday December 27th

What a great day. The first of Nick's five calls started at 7.35am. I was still sleepy. I called him back when I was a little more chirpy. He was happy, he told me about the 'deep and meaningful' conversation he had with his wife. I only hope this all works out. I'm hoping it is only time but not sure at this stage. It is still very much lust. But I do know that we have a very open and honest relationship and hope there is more to it than just the sexual chemistry. Only 13 days to go. I only hope that on the first day I can resist him – keep him waiting! In between phone calls it was very quiet. Hardly anyone in the office between Christmas and New Year. Finished the day with another phone call. I hope this calms down so I can get some work done... ha ha. I'm not really complaining, it is very nice. Nick makes me feel very special. Thank you xx

Thursday December 28th

Another busy day spent on the phone with Nick. Oh that voice. It drives me wild. I really want this man. Can't wait to see him – it will be a little awkward for the first five minutes until that first kiss... or so he tells me. Had my hair cut, not much else to write about. Can't wait til Monday week. It seems like a lifetime to wait but I've been assured that it will be worth waiting for ... yippee !!!

Friday December 29th

Another day spent on the phone. Lucky I don't have a lot of work to do. Nick left his office at lunch time, this is the last time I will get to talk to him for the next few days. He's off camping with the his mates. Oh well, I hope the days go by quickly and I might be a little more productive. Olivia rang to invite me to a party on Sunday night. Not feeling like partying without Nick. It's weird to feel like this but I believe that all I need is a little PATIENCE. Quiet night in.. thinking of you Nick, wish I was camping with you. xx

We had a lot of phone sex, well not quite but there was a lot of time on the phone. It was always during the week. Never on the weekend. I could never contact him, never tell him what I was up to. Never share my thoughts or feelings on the weekends, or when he was at home.

Why? Because I didn't exist and because Rebecca might answer the phone. This was before Nick had a mobile phone. So it was land lines all the way. If you missed a call - you simply missed a call.

Author's Learning:
My diary entries became more intense and detailed at this time. My diary was my 'someone' to share my thoughts and feelings with.

Olivia was my flat mate, along with her boyfriend Logan. Olivia and I talked a lot about my situation. It was always great to have her honest opinion. Ever since we worked together years before we had been able to share everything. I love that about my dear friend Liv!

As the week sped by I had spent a lot of time sorting out plans for our upcoming sales conference. There were 80 people from across Australia travelling to Sanctuary Cove in Queensland. They all needed to have their flights and accommodation booked. It was a lot of long hours and organising but I loved it. It kept me busy and made time fly by when all I wanted to do was have January 8th arrive - like right NOW !

Diary Entry:

Monday January 8th

This day finally arrived, it has been a long few weeks. Work went by really fast considering the anticipation of this evenings activities. Nick's plane was delayed by an hour which meant I got to go home, freshen up and start dinner. Nick arrived while I was talking to Leonie on the phone!

It was very romantic. A bit of a culture shock really – it's weird feeling so special. I just want to run away with him – not used to feeling like this. Dinner was a huge success, dessert is yet to come, so I will be back in a little while – keep you posted.

I was talking to Leonie on the phone when Nick arrived. Leonie was still crazy about Nick. She shared with me her plans to be with him and how much she enjoyed flirting with him. Nick was standing right in front of me. I had to get her off the phone quick. I had to kiss this man.

He just stood there staring at me. He was mesmerized by me. It was strange that he didn't touch me, he just looked. It was like he wasn't allowing himself to touch me (because he shouldn't) - but I knew he would. His hand stretched out and stroked my face. It was killing me. I moved forward - there was no more waiting. We kissed long and passionately. Definitely worth every minute of the wait!

Somehow we managed to eat dinner and it was off to The Stamford, North Ryde to stay the night and have our 'dessert'.

Nick checked into the hotel while I waited in the car. He came out and gave the all clear and we ran to the room. It was our first time.

Since Dan, there had been other relationships. I hadn't been single and innocent that entire time. My sexual references and experiences had definitely improved and I had been enjoying sex more than ever before. But now, because of the feelings I had for Nick, I knew this was going to be extremely passionate and very special.

As we entered the hotel room, Nick calmly placed our bags at the door and took me by the hand. He lead me slowly across to the bed. I wasn't in a "slow" mood but I followed his lead.

With his free hand, he took hold of the bed covers and flung them to the ground. I giggled. The crisp white sheet that covered the mattress became the canvas for us to begin our journey of discovering each other for the first time.

He turned me around so my back was facing the bed. I was expecting him to kiss me again but he pushed me down on the bed. I laughed. It was funny and unexpected.

He slowly lowered himself on top of me. After many divine delicate kisses, his mouth made its way down to my neck. I could feel the buttons on my top being undone. I wanted to speed it up to the good parts but I also wanted to slow it down and enjoy every minute over and over again.

I couldn't wait - I needed him, I wanted to feel him inside me. I pushed him off me, I ripped off his shirt and started to unbuckle his belt. He pulled me back down. He was teasing me. He knew how much I wanted him and I knew how much he wanted me.

It was really heating up, there were two very aroused people in the room, that was for sure.

I was now totally naked. He still had his trousers on but not for long.

He caressed my body all over. There wasn't a part of me that wasn't feeling totally in the moment and in need of more.

My heart pounded with anticipation for his entrance into me. His gentle, yet rhythmic thrusting motion sent me to heights I had never experienced before.

It really was amazing. After all the phone calls and innuendo in the previous weeks, it was no wonder it was truly awesome.

Not just once, twice but three times. I have never felt so loved and been so relaxed sexually. Words just can not explain how I felt. How tender the kisses were. How intense the penetration and the power of orgasms that I experienced. How exciting and wonderful it was to be with this man.

The night seemed to last forever.

We had to be together forever, there was just no other way. This was it. I was finally alive!

Diary Entry:

Tuesday January 9th

Well it's now Tuesday night and all I can say is "Awesome!!!"...... our first night was simply perfect.

I returned to the hotel early, enjoyed a bath and jumped into bed – only to have a body and a good one at that, join me shortly afterwards. We ordered room service and now it's dessert time again! Sometimes life isn't fair – but sometimes it is FABULOUS! I really feel for Leonie, she's at home wishing she was in his bed. Oh how I wish I could share this with her but I know it would really hurt her. So in knowing that, the next few hours are going to be so amazing. Good night xx

Leonie called Nick on a number of occasions during the evening offering to come by and 'keep him company'. It was quite bizarre sitting in the room while Nick took her calls. She wasn't going to let up. Leonie and I were friends. Nick and I hadn't told anyone from the office about our relationship and we certainly couldn't tell Leonie.

After all the calls from Leonie and Rebecca, we finally had time to ourselves. It was different this time. We had our special moments from last night to remember and we had some repeat business to attend to.

That night was special in it's own way. Just lying next to him and having him snuggle up to me was really caring and beautiful. I felt protected, safe and very much in love.

Diary Entry:

Wednesday January 10th

What a night – what a morning. The day went considerably fast. Shipped all the goodies up to the conference venue. Went back to the hotel early then went to dinner with my old work friends (from Dan's days), Dan wasn't there. Dinner was nice until Nick called to say he had to go to the doctors. My heart stopped beating and I couldn't stop worrying about him. I got back to the hotel and he says "we need to talk" – he was joking! He had a reaction to the condoms – too much sex. Phew! It took a while to get all the stress out of my body. Had a great talk – he is just so caring, thoughtful and lovable. Oh if time would just stand still. We stayed up for hours talking, it was just beautiful.

It was definitely a stressful day. Nick had been to the doctor. My heart missed a beat when he told me. What was wrong? Did we break something over the last few nights? Oh, I have never been so concerned about a guy's penis before.

Nick was different in many ways. Nick's was uncircumcised and I had never been with an uncircumcised man before, let alone had sex with one. All the men in my life to date, had had the 'chop'. I really liked it, it was different, he was different.

Diary Entry:

Thursday January 11th

Well the last day ... breakfast was great, had a few hours to waste before getting to work, so we made the most of it. It is nice to see him around the office. I even got to drive him to the airport. Nick admitted that there were no guarantees but he knows he needs to make decisions for himself. It was tough saying goodbye and a bit sad. I chatted to Olivia for an hour and found my smile again. All I have to do is concentrate on the conference and know that in two weeks he will be back for more. Nick if you get to read this, I just want to say, "Please don't scare me like that again and thanks for three great days. The closeness is something I will always cherish. And sorry to say my doona doesn't add up to you"... good night xx

It's amazing just how slowly the weekends passed. They were the lonely times. Constantly thinking of Nick and what he was doing and wondering where he was or who he was with. It was very rare that I would hear from him on the weekends so it was good to have my friends around.

I spent a lot of my spare time with Olivia and Logan. They were a lovely couple and great friends. I was sure they would get married one day and have a zillion kids. Olivia and I both needed to move out of our parents home, so we got a place together in Stanmore, right under the flight path. It was a great spot, even with the aeroplane noise.

Author's Learnings:

Living two lives is hard work. I was living two lives. I had my exciting "weekday" life and my lonely "weekend" life. Nick also had two lives. It was what we got used to and what we accepted. What are you accepting in your life? Do you deserve more? I know now that I certainly do!

Again Nick made it clear that he was ending his marriage with Rebecca. He said it had been coming for some time and that it had nothing to do with me. They had started counselling to help Rebecca deal with the issues around separation.

I spent a lot of time wishing it was over with her already. I longed to have him in my bed every night. Sometimes I felt him beside me, even when he wasn't there. That had never happened to me before!

Diary Entries:

Saturday January 20th

It's Saturday and I've been up for hours. Done all the washing and now sitting on my balcony thinking of Nick. I am so longing to hear his voice. I know he doesn't want to be in his situation, I just wish it was over. Hope I hear from him sometime over the weekend. Can't wait til Monday to tell him that I love him. Hang in there

Nick, well be together soon - only two more sleeps to go. Good night, thinking of you always xx

Monday January 22nd

Well I can't tell you how slow today went by. Spoke to Nick first thing this morning before his flight, gee it's great to hear his voice. I miss him so much on the weekends. The last two days were tough. But he's here now. Seeing him in the office was difficult, we had to meet in the stairwell. Then later, I found my man waiting for me... Now it's my turn. Let's get down to some sexy business. I really am the happiest girl in the world.

Today he was back in town! He had just arrived at the office. We couldn't wait. We met in our secret stairwell. We tried to control ourselves. It wasn't easy. I had been waiting for weeks to see him. It was so good to have him back again.

After work I raced to the hotel. I arrived, parked in the underground car park, looked to make sure I didn't recognise anyone or they didn't recognise me - I snuck through the back entrance up to room 329, hoping he'd been upgraded to a nice hotel suite, not just a standard room. I had spent a lot of time in this hotel.

The door was ajar, he was expecting me. I dumped my bags and stood with a huge smile on my face. Oh, how I had missed him.

I watched him lying in the bed, his long toned body, naked, on the crisp white hotel sheets, waiting for me to join him. I knew this was going to be another great night. I'm sad he would be travelling home the next day to his wife. I planned to enjoy all of him, while he was mine.

On Tuesday night we went out for dinner. What a nice change. We had eaten many meals in hotel rooms. There's only so much room service a girl can take. It was nice to be out in public, being able to show how I felt to the world. After dinner we raced back to the hotel room. Nick made the necessary call to Rebecca and she asked if there was anyone else there. She was getting suspicious. Of course Nick denied it.

Author's Learnings:
That's what you do when you are cheating on your partner... You LIE ! And then you LIE some more, until it becomes second nature... until it forms a habit.

Rebecca's call made me feel bad. Guilt set in fast. It was awful. I started to think 'she's obviously a good person, after all he had chosen her to be his wife. She was certainly not the 'wicked witch' I would like her to be!

We spent a lot of time talking it out. He told me he loved ME but I couldn't wait until this situation was resolved and we could be happy without an extra person in our relationship.

On our last night together I started thinking about the next two weeks waiting for him to come back again. It was starting to hurt. It got harder and harder the longer it went on. Why couldn't it just be over with Rebecca so he could move to Sydney and be with me?

Diary Entry:

Wednesday January 24th

I had heaps of fun today. Talked to Dan for 45 minutes and I didn't even yell at him. It was actually nice to talk to him and discuss the past and the present. His baby boy is now seven months old. His advice to me was "if ever you are pregnant – don't terminate – it's just so amazing". Wow, what a Dad. Couldn't leave work quickly enough to get back to the hotel. Had a sick feeling in my stomach all the way there. Oh I hope Rebecca doesn't show up tonight. She said she might. So here I am, sitting in the hallway outside the room, writing this while Nick is discussing the weather with his wife. The things I do for this man. I just hope my new mobile doesn't ring – it's inside the room. We talked and talked and made love as only we can. It's hard to believe we are so good together. His commitment and dedication to me is sensational. The way he touches me is simply fantastic. I love him. x

The next morning Nick woke me early with a bit of a snuggle. Followed by passionate sex during which we rolled off the bed and onto the floor. We were both in fits of laughter. It was always fun and interesting with Nick.

Afterwards I laid in bed and watched him dress for work, I tried to distract him and get him to come back to bed but he had to go to a meeting. After he left, I got up and took my time getting ready for work. I arrived at work mid morning.

Another office assistant fussed over him most of the day. It was hard to watch but I knew Nick only had eyes for me.

At the end of the day we met in the fire stairs. He promised to come back for me and that we would be together. I hated saying goodbye. Our times together were so fantastic. Tears rolled as I made my diary entry that night. I just had to wait until it was over with Rebecca, then I could have all of him.

I spent Saturday afternoon feeling lonely. I had done my washing and my food shopping. I was angry. I just wanted him for myself. I just wanted to be with him. I felt like I had no control over these feelings of disappointment and hurt.

That night the phone rang. It was Nick. He had snuck away from home to call me. I suddenly felt special. How quickly my mood changed whenever I heard his voice. He apparently just needed to say 'Hi' and that 'he *missed me*'. Suddenly I snapped back to my previous mood and launched at him, "Well do something about it!". Uh-oh! Sometimes, just sometimes, I wished I could keep my mouth shut. Oh well, at least he couldn't question how I felt.

Sunday was another day without my man. I spent the day with my folks. Mum realised that I was especially happy. She asked why and I told her (almost) all about my Melbourne Nick. She was very happy for me. Dad joked that he would not visit me in Melbourne. "Too funny Dad - who said anything about moving to Melbourne?"

I went to bed early in an attempt to make Monday arrive quicker. On Monday I would be able to talk to him again. Oh, I had it real bad.

Monday morning dawned with sweet rewards. Nick called. I got my long awaited call at 7am! Wow it was great talking to him. He wanted me to organise a trip for the two of us at Easter. How exciting! That was only nine weeks away. He admitted that it wasn't fair on anyone to drag the situation out any longer. He was so unbelievably together about the entire thing.

I thought 'He loves me - Yah!'

Diary Entry:

Monday February 5th

This was definitely a day to live thru again. I was in training all day which meant I didn't do any work. Met Olivia at the Airport Sheraton for a drink and Nick met us there too. We only stayed for one drink and it was off to his hotel. It was great to have him back in town again - it will be even better when we don't have to sneak around. We talked for a while and discussed the current status of the situation. All is going OK, it's just hard on him at the moment. I wish I could make it all better. The night was a big success in the sex department. Please note I had my first real 'out of control' orgasm. It was sensational. Wow - can it get any better from here - of course it will. After a fun evening I woke at 4.15am and thinking it was time to get up I woke Nick and made good use of the extra hours. Breakfast arrived, then more sex before heading off to work.

The night was amazing. It started with Nick eating chocolate cake and mango off my stomach, followed by my first ever, best ever full body orgasm. Woo-hoo! One for the record books for me!

Nick used to love watching me as I wrote in my dairy every night. I'm sure he got a buzz out of having our days documented and recorded. Every now and then we would have a reading session, reading back over the past weeks.

My diary became my best friend. It's fun looking back remembering as well as to help me sort through my thoughts and feelings.

Diary Entries:

Monday February 19th

Poor Nick, I stirred him all day from his first call til his last. It was fun. Work was busy. Thinking of Nick at home - tonight is to be the night for telling Rebecca it's all over. Well it's 11:30pm - I'm tired, looking forward to talking to Nick in the morning to see how it went.

Tuesday February 20th

Well last night was not the night. Maybe tonight. Hopefully Nick will be in Sydney from tomorrow night through til next Friday. That would be great.

When Nick was in town he always had to get me an extra key to his room at the Stamford Hotel. He would walk past my desk and discreetly drop off my key. Then he would request another one from the front desk if I wasn't already in our room. The hotel was like my home away from home. We knew the hotel food menu off by heart. The order for food was always the same, to make it look like only one person was eating. One entree, one large main and dessert (of course). Any extra drinks came from the mini bar.

We started getting very good at this game we were playing. I got very clever at packing exactly what I needed and got comfortable living out of a small carry bag.

Diary Entry:

Wednesday May 15th

Was nice to have the day to perv on my man. We spent a great night together. It never ceases to amaze me where he can take my emotions – it was so close to the best yet! Both of us feeling me, quite incredible – very exciting for both of us. Oh to have it more often.

We stopped saying goodbye because saying goodbye was never easy. We would hide out in the fire stairs to have a cuddle and say our 'see you soon's. I would drive him to the airport as often as I could if his flight worked in with work hours.

There were many more trips to Sydney.

Many more days waiting for the right time to tell Rebecca...

A change of surrounding didn't make things easier. I had moved out of the Stanmore townhouse and I lived on my own in Mosman. Being on my own was tough so four months later I moved in with my girlfriend Chloe in Mosman Bay.

Diary Entries:

My Birthday December 16th

What a special day. Work was pretty standard – nothing really exciting, called Nick to thank him for my flowers that I never received. We both got away from work early and I met him at the Parramatta Parkroyal and he gave me my presents; A card, roses and a vibrator. WOW. We had 'a quickie' and then showered and went to Mosman where Chloe cooked dinner for us. It was so special having Nick there. His attention on me all night was so sweet, something I could get used to. Chloe and John gave me a "tickle-me Elmo" so cute. Two vibrating toys in one day... alright! We went back to the hotel and played with my new toys. We had heaps of fun, pity we were so tired. Nick held me close, sorry for not having made his decision sooner. I'm glad he was here for my special "vibrating" day!

Christmas Eve December 24th

Nick called this avo – we talked for 40 mins. I cried. He is so sweet. I wish he was here. I miss him so much. It's weird being in my little house with Chloe's family. It's yuk not having him here. The next four days are going to be tough – will have to find strength to get thru.

Christmas was certainly one of the toughest times.

Two years since it began

January 4 - the day the bomb was dropped.

We sat on the edge of the hotel bed. There was something wrong. I could sense it. He said he needed to tell me something. I was lost and confused. I just wanted him to spit it out.

He finally asked me, "What's the one thing I don't want?" I drew a blank. I don't know, you don't want to die, you don't want cancer, what? Stop playing games and just tell me.

Then I remembered - children! I just looked at him, shook my head and said sadly said "No!"

Finding out Rebecca was pregnant should have been devastating. They were still having sex??? I was not angry - just sad for him. I should have been MAD as hell that he was still sleeping with her.

We laid on that bed together and cried for a long, long time.

Diary Entry:

Monday January 5th

Not a day to remember. Sent Nick a letter after telling him I wanted him to leave me alone for a year. Very sad day. Work didn't help, running around getting a presentation ready for tomorrow's meeting. Nick called to discuss my email this afternoon which produced tears and tears, that flowed all the way home. Chloe was great and very understanding. Had a bath and feel a bit better. Now time to rest these tired sore eyes. Today I lost my best friend, my lover and my soul mate. It is very sad. Oh what I would give for things to change.

5th January "Michelle" wrote:
Dear Nick
Again we go through this... but who really wants to? Not me.

My gut feeling tells me that you need time (without me in your life) to get used to the way life is going to be for you soon. There is another life coming into the world and you should be there 100% or not at all. The way I see it happening is that you will be there - you will get used to the idea and will stay... and I need to start listening to my gut feelings more often.

Me, well I cannot hang around. My life is not happy and I cannot stand it like this anymore. I totally want you in my life and if I cannot pick up the phone to call you at anytime, then I can not be part of this.

The Deal is as follows:
You can call. You cannot visit me or invite me out unless your current status changes... coz we both know what will happen and we will be back in this situation again.

If by December you are single and unattached you are invited to attend my 30th birthday party. It would be great to have you there.

Nick, I wish this did not have to happen.

If you haven't figured it out - I am doing it tough at the moment, sitting here typing with tears in my eyes, it's not a pretty sight - but nothing you haven't seen before.
In closing this letter, I just want to say thanks for a wonderful two years of the best relationship I have ever known and know that you are a fabulous person and I hope somewhere in the future our paths will cross again.

All the best, I hope things turn out fine for you.

Remember you are the only person that can make a difference to your life.

I love you with all my heart and I will miss you totally but we both know this is for the best - set you free and if you come back - and all that stuff.
Bye, love Shelly

Diary Entries:

Friday January 9th

It doesn't seem like a Friday. Work was pretty boring today. Spent a lot of time on the phone tonight with Nick. It is good to talk about everything that is happening. He says he is close to making a decision - but I cannot believe that. He is very understanding of how I feel which is great. He told Trent [fellow work colleague of Nick's] – it's good he has someone to share this with. I sometimes think that he hates me for being so nasty but he says he really understands and knows it's all because of him. He even told me that he loves me – that hasn't happened for a while.

Monday January 12th

Good day. Had things to do, so the day went fast. Nick called to see how my weekend went. I told him about flirting with a 22 year old barman on Saturday night at a party. I was in a good mood, so we had a good chat. He's so supportive of me having a good time. It makes our friendship so special. He will be in Sydney this week sometime. Hope it is not too difficult to see him. Hope he doesn't ask me over. That would not be good. Off to sleep feeling special.

Tuesday January 13th

Nick was in the office today – to my surprise. He rang tonight from his hotel room and we talked for ages. Was nice. Glad I didn't weaken and drive over – go ME !!!

Friday January 16th

Left a message for Nick this afternoon "If you truly believe that I deserve better... then leave me alone!" Pretty nasty – but I know what's going to happen if I allow myself to get too close again. Tomorrow night Nick is going to a team dinner in Mosman with Rebecca. I'm going to be there too. I want to see this situation for *what it really is... Don't really want to but I do want to see the whole picture. Won't feel great about it but it has to be done!*

Late Saturday afternoon I went to Mosman and waited for Nick and Rebecca to arrive. I saw them coming, I was hiding in my car. He would have recognised me and my car if he looked around but he didn't. I felt partly angry, stupid and sad all rolled into one. Angry because I wanted to be the one going to dinner with him. Stupid because I really had been taken for granted. And sad because it had to be over.

After a bit of a low, I picked myself up and felt strong, I felt in control. This relationship was not going to continue down the same track. It couldn't. It had to be over. I had to come up with a plan to make sure of that. I decided to give Nick a time frame of NO contact. Hopefully that would work.

So Monday morning, first thing, I informed Nick that he was no longer allowed to contact me until February. I wanted two weeks of 'me' time.

He was shocked and he was devastated that he had hurt me. I didn't want to see him or hear from him.

He called later in the day. We chatted some more. He was really sorry for hurting me, for making me feel so uncomfortable. He was flying to Sydney in a few days and wanted to take me out for dinner. So much for no contact for two weeks!

On Wednesday he was in the office. He begged me to meet him in the stairwell. So I did. He was very sweet. He was so sorry for the pain he'd caused me at the team dinner. He cried. I cried. I was sad. This is not how it was meant to be. He kissed the tears as they rolled down my cheeks. The more he kissed me, the more I cried.

He wanted to come by and knock on my window that night - I told him he had to wait and we would talk on Thursday.

That was how it was with us. We knew the situation, we knew it was magnetic between us but to end it - was impossible.

I tried so hard to remain strong. The love I had for him was too great. My strength weakened.

Diary Entry:

Thursday January 22nd

WOW what a night. Got home and showered and got ready for our big date. Nick arrived about 6pm. I made him listen to Gina Jeffreys "I want this night to last forever" - while it was playing he held me tight, swaying and tenderly kissed me - it was so beautiful.

We went for dinner in Balmoral. We walked along the beach for a while stopping regularly for a cuddle. In the fish 'n' chip shop he was so affectionate. We then sat under a tree and ate dinner. It was very romantic.

He cried for about an hour - so sad for all he had put me through and how he longs to be with me. We left the beach - came home - packed a bag for me and went back to his hotel. It was very special. We talked and talked for hours. The closeness we feel is really scary. We both know that we need space but he says it wont be for long - but who knows. For the first time he told me (face to *face) that he loves me and I really felt loved. Tonight will never end in my mind. It was... indescribable.*

"So here we go again", I said to myself. It was so difficult to be around him and not be caught up in him, not to be pulled back into the dream of what could be.

Back in the hotel, we took a bath together, not that easy with such a tall guy with long limbs. I thought "he cares, he really does". Having his arms around me and feeling his wet silky skin, was enough for me. This is where I belonged, this is where I wanted to be. I settled for what I could get for now.

We left the bath still dripping wet with no time to get dry and fell onto those crisp white sheets. He placed me underneath him. His hand gently caressed my face before gently moving down my body. I was under his spell. His touch was soft, slow and purposeful.

The night was filled with passion and love making. I felt sorry for him, feeling sorry for hurting me. It was a vicious cycle. We woke after a few hours sleep to have more sweaty sex and then off to work. How I ever got through those days, I can't imagine.

Nick returned to Melbourne and I was alone and sad once more. I just hated not having him here. I got busy with my work. Anything to stop my brain from thinking.

Dad called to invite me to spend a nice holiday with him, Mum, my brother and his wife in Fiji for 10 days. I couldn't think of anything worse. Imagine being on a beautiful island, on a beautiful beach knowing I would spend the whole time wishing Nick was with me. No, I couldn't do that to myself. Sorry Dad.

I booked tickets to see a comedy show and Nick and I were going as a couple, out in public. It should have been a great night. That was the plan anyway, until Rebecca called just as we arrived and finally found a car park. I felt she was onto him. I felt she knew something Her intuition must have been screaming at her.

Nick spent the next 48 minutes (the longest 48 minutes of my life) talking to her and making her understand that everything was okay. Luckily we had allocated seating or we would have been left out in the cold.

We finally got in to see the show just as it had started. It took a while for Nick to chill out and enjoy it. It was great to see him have a laugh and enjoying himself. He had a great sense of humour. Afterwards we left the theatre and drove home (back to the hotel) to yet another passionate night together.

In that department - he never let me down. No matter what was going on around us, he could always turn on the charm in bed and make me feel like his princess.

Diary Entry:

Saturday February 21st

Weird to have Nick here. Slept in a little. We had to do some organising for the party tonight. We drove up to Pittwater to look at buying Nick a boat to live on when he moves to Sydney. Then he went off to have dinner with Trent and the guys. We met up again at the party. We had a major misunderstanding and it was not very nice at all. Home at 4:00am, made up and tried to get some *sleep. I hope I never have to go through that again. It wasn't nice. What was nice was having him here all day and being with him... planning our future.*

Nick stayed for a weekend!

Amazingly so. Nick was in town for a Friday and a Saturday night and he stayed at my place. Bliss!!

Friday night was a night to celebrate. He was staying in my bed. He was in my house. Even better news was he'd just received a National Manager promotion. YIPPEE ! He would definitely be spending even more time in Sydney and may even be based here. I was getting closer to my dream. Closer to having him here all the time. Just one person stood in the way... or should I say two!

When Nick wasn't in Sydney, I would often go out with my new flat mate Chloe. Chloe had been through a horrible marriage and as a result of her leaving her husband, we became good friends. Our plan was to grow old together, she was going to be Ethel and I was going to be Beryl. We shared fun girly times together.

We often went out with her brother Jackson and his friends; Aiden and Ashley. Aiden was a cutie. One night we went to the movies and Aiden showed up in a suit. That did it for me. What is it about a man in a suit? I turned to jelly. It was terrible, I felt so vulnerable.

Diary Entry:

Friday March 13th

Maybe it was because it was Friday 13th but Nick and I had a huge fight tonight. Why do we do that? Why do we hurt each other - it doesn't make any sense. I hate the fact that we do that.

The weekend was long. I didn't hear from Nick. I felt horrible that we had fought and that he hadn't contacted me. I hated having tension between us.

I finally heard from him on Monday. He said, 'Everything was fine, he wasn't mad with me at all.'

If I had been able to contact him on weekends, I would have known he wasn't mad instead of feeling awful for two whole days. Being the 'other woman' really sucked. It was such a roller coaster ride of emotions.

Diary Entry:

Wednesday March 18th

He's back! and what a night it was. Wouldn't trade places with anyone in the entire world. Just when I thought our 'love-life' should be getting a bit predicable, he turns it into the best ever. I love him so much.

With six weeks to go until Rebecca was due to give birth to his baby, I started getting uneasy. I took some time off work and flew to the Sunshine Coast to get my head together. Nick reassured me many times that he wasn't at all thrilled about having a child. He called to say he wanted to be with me. The right words always came out of his mouth.

When I returned from my holiday I was scheduled to undergo laser surgery on abnormal cells in my cervix. It wasn't fun. I went in alone and came out alone. I felt the entire procedure. It was painful physically and psychologically.

Nick arrived back in town the following day - caring and supportive. We couldn't have sex for six weeks. This didn't phase him in the slightest. He just wanted to be with me, to hold me and to care for me and I wasn't complaining.

Saturday March 18th - Rachelle Leigh Watkinson was born. It felt weird. Even weirder was the name they chose for her. Starting with R for Rebecca - ending in Elle like Michelle. On top of that her middle name was Leigh, same as mine, even spelt the same. I did not cope well with this news.

I spent the following days pampering myself. I was feeling very 'yuck'. I decided I should start a new hobby, to do something regularly for me. I started playing tennis at Evergreen tennis courts on Saturdays to help fill up the void on my weekends.

I hated the feelings of insecurity, loneliness and sadness. Nick assured me that I would not lose him. I wasn't so sure, I had waited so long.

In the following weeks Nick didn't travel to Sydney. He's stayed close to Rebecca and Rachelle to make sure all was okay. Understandable I guess but I was feeling used and cheap. I just hoped this feeling would pass.

Author's Learnings:
UP AND DOWN feelings and emotions. Uncontrollable and vulnerable. When you are the 'other' woman, it's not your relationship - it's their's... it's never on your terms or in your control. You have to take what you get and you don't get to ask for much more than that.

Diary Entry:

Monday May 4th

It's over! Spoke to Nick first thing this morning and he totally understands. It's been going on way too long and it's just all too much. Work was busy and I was suffering horrible period pain and was crabby. Nick called again tonight - very friendly and caring. Cant wait to see him on Wednesday night. We didn't talk for long, get the feeling something is going down.

I saw Nick on Wednesday night. I was angry. It took a long time for me to feel calm. We talked for ages. He still wanted me to help him find a place to live and where I could be with him. I found it all too hard.

On Saturday night I was home alone again. I wrote my final good byes.

Sent via email
On 11/May 8:34 AM, "Michelle" wrote:
Dearest friend,
Here I go again, sharing my feelings with you. I warn you up front this is probably not what you want to hear at this time.

Our love and friendship has to come to an end. I am unable to continue in this situation. Nick, you know it's been tough on me for some time and after sharing Wednesday and Thursday with you, I know this has to end. I remember comments like "it will happen" and "you miss me' but I also heard the "it will be another six months" ... sorry I am not going to wait, for the one thing I have wanted for years.

You and I have been through a lot. Probably more than most people go through in a relationship. I don't regret any of it. Especially our last two nights together. You said that you didn't want me to be 'bitter and twisted' towards you. I fear this most of all. It has started and we know that the more time that goes by, the worse it will get. Oh, and I am glad that I was able to remind you how sexy I am. It gave me great pleasure for you to give me the chance to remind you of that.

If you re-read my last letter of January you will see that even though we continued our relationship, things are still the same - if not worse than back then. Nick you promised me things which I believed in. I will NOT hold you to those promises... I know that you will, one day, be strong enough to make the right decisions but they are your decisions, <u>you</u> have to make them.

It wasn't until this morning when I finally unpacked my bag that it hit me that I deserve more of a quality-filled life. I deserve to have someone in my life that is willing to give up everything to be with me because they love 'me' and want to spend every available minute with 'me'... don't get me wrong I do understand where you are at, I don't hate you for that... but I need more.

Nick I'm sorry for the many times we have been through this and this time may seem like just another to add to the list but you have to believe me - it's not. I will not meet up with you to discuss this, for that will only put off again for another few months. We will probably run into each other in the office, please excuse me, in advance, if I choose to ignore you.

You know this is not what I want. So many things have been making it so much clearer lately... at the movies last week, a line was "Choose ONE person and make it work". I guess this is what it all comes down to. At the moment you feel you have to choose your family, this is the right thing to do. But I remember you saying you should have left after you found out Rebecca was pregnant. You still have to choose even though you feel the choice has been made for you.

Nick, you said last week that you want me to be happy and when you come for me you want me to be the Shelly you knew and loved and is happy... I'm not that person right now and I want to be that Shelly too, that has a sense of peace inside. I want and need that so much.

Maybe our time will come, maybe not. I'm not waiting for that day... I want to share my feelings with the world - I want everyone to know when I'm in love and not have to hide it. Yes the secrecy was fun but enough is enough. I think we are both

passed the 'fun' element of it now. I want to go
out and not feel guilty or ashamed for flirting.
I guess there's not much else to add, I'm sorry but
you are right - it's time and I have to walk away
and you have to let me. This will hopefully stop
all rumours about us which will make life better
for both of us. Nick this time I feel really
strong and hope you do the right thing and help me
stay strong.

I don't want to set any rules, I don't
think that's fair. I have receipted this
email so I know you have received it.
I do love you a lot and look forward to talking to
you soon,
Til then,
Shelly xxx

Nick called a few days later and I knew I had made the right decision.
It was tough to do but I had no choice. What sort of a life was I
leading anyway. We'd talked about the entire situation over and
over but nothing changed.   I kept my distance as much as possible.
I had to be true to me.

Over the next month. I started going out on 'real' dates with other
men. I enjoyed many dates with Chloe's brother's friend Aiden. We
had a great friendship. I remember one night I was sound asleep
and Aiden dropped in to say "Hi" on his way home from work. He
kissed me on the forehead and said "Go back to sleep, I'll see you
tomorrow." I knew I had to get back into the dating world quickly
or I would find myself back in Nick's arms again.

Aiden worked for the navy. We would often attend functions at the navy bases around Sydney. He was based in Mosman which was so close it was scary. Our friendship grew strong over many months.

Chloe was also dating a 'navy' guy. So the four of us spent many nights out on the town or entertaining at our place. We would often have a house full of navy recruits, both guys and gals. It was always a lot of fun. I was having fun. I was happy and I was not thinking of Nick.

Aiden used to sneak me off to the kitchen (in the back of the house) so he could have a cuddle or two or three. It was so nice to muck around and have a bit of fun and not have to hide. He would lift me up on the kitchen bench so he didn't have to break his neck to kiss his 'short blondie'.

Diary Entry:

Thursday June 4th

Met up with Nick after work at the Stamford Hotel for a drink. It was nice to sit and chat. Saying goodbye was really hard. I cried all the way home. It finally has hit me that it's over. Went home and patched up my face and went out to dinner with Chloe and the guys. Glad I didn't sit at home alone and feel sad.

I would often see Nick in the office. On occasion I would go and meet him for a drink but I never went over to visit or to stay with him.

Nick called one evening as Aiden and I were on the way out to the video store. Aiden asked who I was talking to. I told him it was Nick, he said "He must really love you if he still calls you". It was sweet of him to understand. We talked about it for hours later that night and it felt great to share my "Nick" story with him.

Aiden knew how to make me laugh. One night all he wanted to do was sing nursery rhymes. We stayed up til 2:30am singing and being silly. It was just what I needed.

Author's Learnings:
The universe sends people into our lives just when we need them. I believe this to be true of Aiden. He was my breath of fresh air - 'just what the doctor ordered'.
There's a great poem ... Reason, Season and Lifetime that explains this so well.

On his next trip to Sydney, Nick called to invite me over to his hotel. I turned him down! He said he was just teasing and testing me. What he really wanted was to talk about was Rebecca. I felt relieved to be one step away from his situation. I finally felt like I had some control, I felt I was finally letting go.

The first time Aiden claimed me as his girlfriend in front of his navy mates made me feel really special. Then sadly we got the news that Aiden and some of his mates was shipping out in seven weeks. We made many memories together in those first weeks after receiving the news. One Saturday afternoon we took funny photos together doing 'squooshy' faces. We always had great belly laughs together.

Soon after we decided to cool off our relationship. It was hard but we knew we were getting closer and it would be more difficult to let go, the longer our relationship went on.

After I shared with Nick that Aiden was leaving, Nick asked me out to dinner.

We went to City Extra at Circular Quay. We talked about Aiden and how good he had been for me. We also chatted about Nick's new baby daughter and how things were uncomfortable between he and Rebecca. We decided we could just be friends and enjoy time together.

I was missing Aiden's fun and laughter, so I spent time together with Nick. It was nice to be his friend after years of trying to be more than his lover.

Diary Entries:

Tuesday August 4th

Bad day. Really flat-out at work. Off to see an early movie with Chloe and Aiden. I was pretty sad. Dropped Aiden at the base and called Nick. I sat at the end of our street for ages talking to him. Cried about the world being a horrible place. Nick promised to call back in half an hour... two hours later and I'm still waiting. I hate waiting.

Wednesday August 5th

Went to work. Nick called on my way into work. He was very low. Rebecca had called him for an hour and a half after I called last night - no wonder he never rang back. We met in the fire stairs at 9:30am for a cuddle which made us both feel a whole lot better. Aiden called tonight, I'm going to miss him. He's become more than a great friend.

I spent another evening with Nick. We had a delicious dinner together and I went home early. It felt good being so strong.

Diary Entries:

Saturday August 29th

Aiden's birthday today. We went out to the Rattle Snake Grill at Neutral Bay. We had a great night. I'm going to miss these Navy guys when they ship out next week. They really know how to have a good time.

Friday September 4th

Aiden called three times to make sure I was going out with him tonight. I picked him up on the way home and walked in to find the biggest, beautiful bunch of flowers waiting for me. We went to the City then afterwards Aiden wanted to come in and hold me one more time... I sent him home. It's hard to imagine life without him around. He's been important to me over the last few months. I have a card to give him tomorrow... I know it's going to be a tough day.

Saturday September 5th

Aiden rang to wake me this morning. I got up and dressed, picked him up along with all his bags. He looked extremely handsome in his uniform. We arrived at the airport and as I got out of the car, Aiden put a card on my seat. It was beautiful. Tears fell from my eyes -

oops! Sat at the airport for a while and talked. It was sad to say goodbye. He walked down to the plane and then he looked back one more time. I know that he cares deeply for me. I just know it.

Aiden's card read:

You showed me much of myself I didn't know existed. You made me very happy and I will miss you more than you would probably imagine. Don't hesitate to call me if you need, don't hesitate to visit, please feel free. As to the future we shall see, for I will always be, your friend, Aiden. XXOO

Then followed - **The Worst Week of my Life!**

Aiden had been gone now for a few days and I was slowly getting used to him not being around. I missed his laughter.

Nick was in town. I went over and had dinner with him to celebrate his 33rd birthday. It was nice to chat and talk about all that was going on at work with the company take over, the upheaval and the repositioning of staff. It made a change from talking about Rebecca or about us!

Diary Entry:

Friday September 11th

It was a Big day. Chloe's last day at work today. We went out for lunch to celebrate. Tammy arrived from the Melbourne office and will be staying with me all week. We have an action packed week planned. Went to the Oaks Hotel after work and there were a lot of interstate people there.

Half way thru the night, Tammy and I walked down to the supermarket to get some camera batteries. On the way she told me that we could compare some 'who we've slept with stories'... She then confesses she's slept with Nick. My Nick !

Tammy didn't know about me and the three years on again, off again relationship that I was having him... and how much I was in love with him... The rest of the night was just awful. Tim started buying me Zambucca shots and the rest is a BIG blur.

We went into the Q Bar in Darlinghurst but only stayed a while because I couldn't stop crying. Out there on the dance floor Tammy decided to take me home.

Tammy, Chloe and I stayed up and we talked it through for hours. They are the best friends a girl could have. It just feels like years ago when I found out about Dan. Why didn't he tell me... Why did I have to find out this way...

That was the end for me. I was so disappointed in him. I was so angry and upset by the news. It apparently only happened once, ages ago, when Nick and I had broken up but he knew Tammy and I were good friends. He must have known I would find out. Tammy and I talked almost everyday at work. She was the Sales Coordinator in Melbourne and we shared so much of our lives in our conversations.

How could I look at him now. Why hadn't he just told me? I had accepted so much from him already. I had forgiven so much - I loved him.

After I calmed down, Tammy explained it happened after a big night out and there had been lots of alcohol involved. That wasn't great but I understood how alcohol can play a part. But still, why hadn't he told me? I knew everything else there was to know - didn't I ??? Should I be questioning more?

Nick called Saturday afternoon. Calling on a weekend was unusual but I guess he thought there was a lot on the line if I found out. I was very calm considering. He knew by the tone in my voice that I knew his little 'secret'. He said "I told Tammy not to tell you". I couldn't believe he was still trying to cover it up. Would he have ever told me?

He was sorry!

I wish I could have been really mad. I wish I could have yelled and screamed at him but I couldn't. I still loved him.

At the end of our conversation, he shared with me that he had accepted a job offer in Sydney.

After everything we had been through, I couldn't believe he chose that moment to share this news with me!

On the day of Nick's birthday I sent text messages and we talked for ages. Why could I not be angry with him?

Two days later - Nick resigned his current position.

Triangle Side 2

Diary Entry:

Wednesday September 16th

Nick came over at 6:30pm to take me out for dinner with roses and a sorry card. We cried. We left for dinner. Dinner was OK.

Home for a cuddle (at my place). Tammy came home (as she was staying with me) and came and sat on the end of the bed. Nick was embarrassed. Then Rebecca calls and asked if he's having an affair... the day can't get any better. Nick left and went back to his hotel. Tammy and I sat up for hours talking about this bizarre triangle of all triangles – or should I say square of all squares!

Nick's card read:

Shelly, I'm so sorry I broke our 'pact'. I hope you can forgive me, as you mean a lot to me. I really look forward to making it up to you. Love Nick x

Diary Entry:

Thursday September 17th

Rebecca calls first thing this morning and asks for a divorce. Wow.

Tammy and I spent the day in Palm Beach having a lovely day. Collected real estate papers for Nick along the way. Took them over to him tonight. We were having a nice night until Rebecca called and they talked for an hour and a half. Apparently someone called her a month ago to say he was having an affair. Who would do something like that. I stayed the night and tried to get some sleep. It was not a nice evening. He was so concerned about her.

The next day Tammy helped me purchase a gorgeous sapphire and diamond ring. It was a promise ring to myself that I would be strong and make good choices for me. A reminder not to let anyone treat me badly ever again.

Nick went home to face Rebecca and her allegations. I didn't hear from him for days. I was so concerned.

That weekend Nick called while Tammy and I were having breakfast. Everything was fine. He was moving out. He also shared with me that his test results were back and he had been diagnosed with chronic fatigue. No wonder, he had so much stress going on in his body!

The following week was action packed.

I was offered a new job at a large soft drink company. It was very exciting.

Nick moved into an apartment in Sydneyand spent his first night on his own.

We talked about our future and decided one day at a time was the best right now.

I resigned from my current role and took a holiday up the coast.

My new life was starting! Nick was able to call anytime he pleased. I could call him anytime I needed to too.

One day at a time. One day at a time!

Diary Entry:

October Thursday 15th

Got up early and drove back to Sydney. Ten days alone in Coffs Harbour has been great. Got home, unpacked and got ready for a big night out with Nick. He called to say he had to go out to dinner with his new boss and that he would call me later. I was not happy. I undressed and sat around in my bathrobe waiting for him to call. The call came at 10pm. In the car and off to the city for a night of fulfilling fantasies. We had heaps of fun. I must love him a lot, oh, I do! Finally I have my man!

The days went by. I had a new job that was keeping me busy. Nick also had his new role in Sydney. He was still commuting to and from Melbourne every week. I enjoyed staying with him when he was in town.

Nick and Rebecca had started counselling again. He was living in Sydney on the weekdays and flying back to Melbourne for the weekends. So, I still didn't have my man. My weekends were still on my own!

Diary Entry:

October Saturday 31st

Up early and on the road. Looking for a new home for Nick. He's loving the Manly area. Close enough for him to commute to the city every day. How exciting having him so close by. It will be really different now.

Mum and Dad wanted to plan a 30th birthday party for me. I didn't really want one. Who would I invite? Nick probably would be in Melbourne. "Just forget it" I told them. "We'll just do a family baked dinner, that will be lovely."

Diary Entry:

November Sunday 8th

A very relaxing day. Mum and Dad came over for lunch. Talked to Nick tonight but feeling like we are drifting apart. We don't have much to talk about anymore.

November Thursday 12th

Back to the city tonight. It was very romantic. We watched a movie together. It was quite funny. The night was again awesome in the sex department... just when I thought we had lost it...

Tennis was hotting up. I was invited to a BBQ on Sunday and was very eager to meet new people away from my work place. I couldn't wait. Someone forgot to tell me that part of the BBQ was watching the Bathurst Car race, not my cup of tea! I spent most of the time out by the pool chatting to other people who were also not interested in the race. I didn't mind, I was meeting new people and that was important.

The weeks seemed to fly by. I was getting tired of being rejected by Nick for one reason or another. Work functions. Counselling sessions. His Health. There was always something else and not me.

I occupied my time with my new job and my tennis social activities were increasing. It felt good to be part of something fun, part of a gang.

Diary Entry:

Monday December 7th

Feeling unwanted. Returned Nick's apartment key. It felt right to put the key on the table, turn and lock the door behind me.

Friday December 11th

Finally spoke to Nick. Told him this is it. Over, don't contact me again. He's not impressed but said 'If that's the way you feel' ... WOW, is that how much I'm worth fighting for. I was upset by that. I know he's going thru hell, so his mood is probably warranted. The fight is over!

My fight to win was finally over.

Moral of Side 2:

So why did I not wait just that little bit longer. Waiting is exhausting. I was tired of hoping. Tired of longing for what always seemed - just out of my reach. I knew what real love was. To forgive someone no matter what they did or didn't do. With Nick, I knew that love.

Sneaking around being the 'other' woman can be fun. It certainly can fulfil many sexual desires and pleasures however the lonely times in between visits are just that - lonely. The percentage of men that leave their wives in the end is so low... not even worth counting!

Remember - life is short, you get just one chance. I finally tuned in and listened to my intuition. I moved on after three long years of waiting. I believe living a double life can only last so long.

Dr Phil says "the chances of a relationship, that starts with infidelity, to end up happily every after, is like winning the lottery." Source: 2010. Affair Intervention

What happened next:

Nick did leave Rebecca. He overcame his chronic fatigue and got himself well again. He obeyed my request and I never heard from him.

Olivia and Logan married and have two beautiful children.

Aiden found true love in Cairns and married his sweetheart.

Tammy and I remained friends.

I continued playing tennis on Saturdays and hoped to find 'love-all' on the tennis courts.

TIME

Do you really know
Do you really care
The thoughts I feel for you
My love that is so rare

It isn't just a fad
An infatuated fling
It's love from deep inside
And all my love I bring

I give it all to you
Without the bounds of time
For I shall love you always
Although you'll not be mine

You're someone very special
A lover with no regret
And when this life is over
You're the one I won't forget

Don't easily forget me
In your life ahead
I'm with you every moment
Just remember what I said

I'll love you now and always
And keep you near my heart
Our thoughts will be together
They'll never ever part

Although our paths must wander
And you'll go yours, I mine
I'll love you til eternity
Until the end of time.

Written by Big Dan
(Fellow Freesia picker)

TRIANGLE SIDE 3

The time has come. Tonight is the night. At 6:30pm he is meeting me in the bar of my hotel. This time I'm the one cheating on my husband.

My stomach has never churned so much or felt so much anticipation.

He arrives, he comes towards me at the bar. He doesn't speak. His hand softly touches my face. His thumb slightly brushes my bottom lip. My lip gets pulled down, he moves closer. His breath is warm and the thought of his lips on mine shudders my body.

The seconds tick by, it seems like forever. Slowly his lips approach mine, his lips are soft and ready to devour me. I feel guilty, I want to be with him and I don't.

I was now 38 years old. It was 2007.

So, there must be a third side to the Temptation Triangle.

Ten years have passed and I am married to Sean. We had been married for six years and have two adorable children.

"Can I say I have cheated on my husband and fulfilled all positions on the triangle?"

When Sean and I met I was ready for a real relationship. After three years with Nick's on again off again sneaking around as his 'other' woman, I was ready. Ready to show the world that I was capable of an open air, in public, being committed to someone kind-of relationship.

I wasn't going to be the 'other' woman anymore, I was READY for the real deal!

Meeting Sean, shortly after breaking up with Nick for the final time, was just the fresh start I needed.

He was amazing. Strong, surfy, sporty, good looking, younger than me (just a little bit) and a handyman who could fix anything. Yes I know what you're thinking, "keep this one".

We met whilst playing social tennis on Saturdays. We laughed and joked at how bad I was at the game. He came every week with his friend Leon. Leon was a classic Italian from a very large family. Always having fun and always making us laugh.

Here's how our love-all on the courts began...

Diary Entries:

Friday January 1st - New Years Day

Quiet day after last night. Looking forward to tennis tomorrow.

Saturday January 2nd

Well, well - got up and had breakfast - got ready for tennis - did my hair and bought a new sun visor - looked great - of course! Sean was there today with his friend Leon. They are great guys and Sean is an exceptional cutie. After tennis we went to the pub for drinks, I heard him say to Judy, "I've never seen Michelle do anything but smile." He called me "Blondie", then Leon wanted to know my surname and my address and when we all left Leon also asked for my phone number and said they would drop in to see me tomorrow. Later Dad called to remind me it was Uncle Ronald's 80th Surprise Party tomorrow... oh no. HELP! Don't know how I'm going to do this but as usual everything will work out - I can't wait to tell Tammy.

LOOK OUT - THIS CHICK's ON FIRE !

Sunday January 3rd

Tiring day - went to Campbelltown. Was weird meeting relatives I never knew I had. It was a very hot day. Glad the GTI has air con. No news from Sean or Leon, glad but disappointed. Oh well - at least I will be able to hassle them when I next speak to them. Off to bed early - work tomorrow.

Monday January 4th

Absolutely FAB day! Back at work which wasn't great but that didn't stop me calling Sean tonight and hassling him about not dropping in yesterday. We talked for about 20minutes - I couldn't shut him up. His surname is Stuart and he is a cabinet maker - he knows Annalise **(an old work colleague)** they were in the same art class together in high school... scary small world. He promised to call me before Saturday and suggested we do something Saturday night or Sunday morning - YIPEE! The rest of the day I just floated around.

Thursday January 7th

LOVE IS IN THE AIR!

What a great day! Sean called and chatted for ages. He is a major cutie... He is booking somewhere for us to go for dinner on Saturday. Oh no, what will I wear ? Hope the hair goes right - too many things to think about... He was shocked when I told him I remembered his birthday and he said that he's wasn't very good at remembering dates so I will have to remind him when it's my birthday in December... hope he's still around then.

WOW - I am so impressed, I can't wait to tell the girls at work tomorrow... I feel so special. I am really happy - I can't believe he can chat for such a long period of time. It amazes me. Stay tuned for Saturday...

Friday January 8th

I walked around on cloud nine all day. It was great - all the girls were jealous and so excited for me. Finished work and had a few drinks after work with the girls. Time for a snooze - big day tomorrow - have to dye hair, shop for outfit/shoes, play tennis, go on a date & hopefully get some sleep...

Saturday January 9th

WOW - I'm speechless... firstly before 'the date'... I went and bought some new pants for tonight and some new tennis gear. Got to tennis early - I didn't recognise Sean at first - he wasn't wearing his cap and yes he does have all his hair. During tennis he asked if I was still OK about tonight. Judy overheard and asked me 20 questions. At the pub afterwards Sean sat along side me and the looks he gave me were FAB! His eyes and his cheeky grin are just so beautiful.

I got changed at Mum & Dad's on the Plateau. Sean picked me up at 6:45pm, met Mum and Dad, he said I looked great - Dad checked out the Subaru and did the bloke thing and kicked the tires. Sean opened the car door for me - too sweet! Mum was all smiles.

We got to Stella Blu at Dee Why and we had a table in the back. He talked all the way thru dinner - it was great. Surprisingly I didn't say much at all. After dinner we drove to Manly and we walked the entire length of the beach and down the Corso for ice-cream and then back. He held my hand the whole way - very nice indeed. We almost got back to the car and it started to rain. Oh no... the hair had looked so good. Sean drove me back to the Plateau to get my car and he pulled me over for a quick kiss good night. It was nice – he asked if he could call me after his bike ride in the morning and come over and visit. WOW... I said yes of course. I AM REALLY HAPPY...

Sunday January 10th

Woke up and was summoned to Chloe's room. I sat on the end of the bed and had to give a minute by minute account of last night. Finally talked to Sean just before 2pm. He came over and we walked to Cremorne Point and back. Chloe met Sean and approved of course. 10/10.

Sean left but I just wanted to kiss him forever...

He wants me to meet his Mum & Dad next weekend – HELP!

I am very attracted to this guy – I just can't believe I never get a word in – he has some great stories, it's great. I just wish I could over come these nerves when he's around. WOW... just imagine the girls at work tomorrow...

Monday January 11th

The girls were ecstatic. Work was busy. Came home at 5pm... couldn't wait to get out of there – not feeling well. Organised tickets for Friday night to the tennis. Going with Sean, Chloe, Lachlan and Yvette. Should be a lot of fun. I can't wait to see Sean again.

Sean wants to keep 'us' a secret at tennis and see how they all talk... he's talked to Leon about 'us' and Leon thinks it's all very cool.

Mum called to see how Saturday night went – she thinks he's beautiful... It all seem too good to be true... this is FAB !

Friday January 15th

I wish I had words to express the excitement I feel inside. Sean has just left and I want him so badly. We just had the most beautiful night ever. We went to the Adidas International. He had such a great time - he chatted the whole time which was funny. He went off and bought food without even asking. He's just so sweet. He calls me Michelle which I think is just lovely - but no-one knows who he is talking about. He's coming to Shania **(Twain)** concert with me in Feb... Wow forward planning.... he likes to be on time.... he likes the oldies music... he's just PERFECT for me.

When we got home, I dragged him into the bedroom and threw him on the bed. He blushed... That last kiss tonight standing outside his car leaning in the window was pure MAGIC. Life is great - and I'm very happy indeed... and so is he.

Saturday January 16th

I'm his BABE!

... and the happiest girl on this earthly planet. Tennis was fun - actually had Sean as a partner and kicked butt - score 6-2. Was a lot of fun. We went to the pub and held hands under the table and when we both got up to leave the others went woooooooohoooo. Then Leon got up and said I'm going with them - they all laughed. Sean gave me a kiss near my car and said I'll see you tonight. We had the house to ourselves. I can smell him on my skin. oops... back to the diary... we had dinner and watched 'Good Will Hunting', then some tennis. We stayed on the couch for a while, we had great cuddles and fabulous kisses, his words ' I don't ever want you to forget you're my Babe'... and then he left, he said 'don't be sad, we have plenty of time...' He's just too good to be true. I'm am crazy about him ...and it's only been a few days really.

Sunday January 17th

Today was meant to be a quiet day – Peter B (old dancing friend) called at 9:30am and said he was visiting. Sean called after his bike ride to check if everything was OK for tonight. He gave me directions and thanked me for being so nice last night. WOW...

Peter came by and we chatted for three hours about life before he left and I had to get ready to meet Sean's parents. The night went really well. He is so proud of me – I just feel it. He even kissed me in front of his family which was nice. Brian, Megan, Trista and Jarrod. He had done the full de-brief on me coz they knew everything about me, except for the fact I want to rip all his clothes off.... Megan even asked me if I would want to get married and have children – that was a bit weird.

Good night – I'm on top of the world. He asked if seeing him for the last three nights was good or bad --- I said EXCELLENT..!

Friday 22nd – Saturday 23rd January

Well at this time 1:05am on Saturday morning, Sean is playing with my hair while I'm writing this. We have just watched my favourite movie 'Only You' with Robert Downey Jr. and now we are safely under the mozzie net and he is caressing my back. Tonight is very special and I wouldn't want to be anywhere else in the world.

It's so nice and tomorrow I will fill you in with all the details after I wake up next to this extremely cute guy. I still can't believe this is really happening...

Well it really is happening and I feel like I'm waiting for the bubble to burst – he's serious about us and told me that his boss, Ed, reckons we will get married – WOW. Sean must have said something to make him come to that conclusion. Last night was just beautiful and waking up with him was lovely. We didn't have sex, it was just beautiful to be next to him. I've searched for years to find someone who knows what touch is all about. My body aches for him. I know he is extremely passionate and loving.

He was telling me this morning one of his favourite songs is (I) Don't Know Much but, I held my hand over his mouth but when I took it away he said 'but I know how to love you'... WOW. **(Song by Linda Ronstadt and Aaron Neville)** It was our special moment.

I'm still feeling that it's too perfect and I should push him away but he said he wouldn't let me.

Sunday January 24th

Sean is on his way over with rolls and chicken... too cute.

Missed having him here last night but glad to have some sleep – 11 hours in total. Can't wait to see him again – my Babe! This is moving all a bit fast but I'm happy about it. He's invited me out tomorrow night with all his friends... should be fun...

Monday January 25th

Worked today – it went really slowly... I couldn't wait til 6pm... got dressed in record time. Looking fab in my long black halter neck dress. Sean picked me up – he too has good dress sense. Dinner was OK, lots of fun at the Teppanyaki Restaurant throwing food around... We then went to Darling Harbour and to the Opera House and then decided to ditch his friends and come home.

We did get some sleep and a sleep in tomorrow is definitely on the cards.

AUSTRALIA DAY

Waking up next to Sean is something I want to do forever. I hope to remember this night for a long time. Our friendship / relationship is getting better all the time... It's just so............ Words just can't explain this.

And that's how our story began...

I decided to leave this part of my diary 'as is'. Original excerpts, so you can see how great our relationship was right from the start. The perfect guy, the perfect time, the perfect relationship.

Sean appeared in my life when I was ready. I had been the other woman for too long. This was my time. I was over Nick, but had I really let him go? I never forgot him. The dream of our life together was difficult to let go.

Sometimes I would search for him on the internet. I would Google his name and never find him. There were plenty of men out there with the same name but not my Nick. An old work colleague told me he was working for a company in Melbourne but I never did manage to track him down. I finally let him go.

Sean and I socialised a lot with our tennis friends. We went on car rally weekends, played competition tennis and went to loads of BBQs and group dinners.

After a year of dating, Sean and I bought a top floor apartment in Manly Vale and moved in together. The pressure was now on to have children. I didn't want children, I knew I was past that stage in my life. If I'd had children when I was married to Dan, that would have been fine. After constant discussions and requests, I gave in. ONE child! "I will give you one child" I remember saying to Sean.

Years later, we married and two children were born, a second shortly after the first. So my life had completely changed. I was now a 'stay at home mum' looking after two small children. WHO would have thought? I would never have imagined this would or could have become my life.

I started an 'at home business' so I could stay home and raise our children. We had many fun times, parties, holidays which created many happy memories along the way.

Often I would come across my box of old diaries hidden under my bed and my mind would wander back and wonder what happened to those relationships that changed and shaped my life.

News of a High School Reunion got my mind racing even more. Where was Dan? Where was Nick? What were they doing? Where did they go? How did their lives turn out? I tried again to track them both down but I had no success. I don't know what I would have done had I found them anyway.

As the years passed and the children grew up, they started pre-school and then 'big' school. We settled into our life's routine and cruised through the years. We enjoyed many weekends at the beach. Sean would always be off surfing or bike riding with me and the kids tagging along.

Our relationship was fine. Sean never chose to argue with me, nor I with him, so it made for a peaceful existence and then I met Harry.

I wasn't looking for anything extra in my life. I was content in my world with Sean and the children... or was I?

Harry was a professional staging guy that I met at a seminar weekend in the Blue Mountains. We just clicked from the beginning. We stayed up late each night talking and laughing together.

He ran his own business setting up conferences and trade shows for corporate companies and he loved his job, travelling around Australia. He enjoyed morning swims and long evening walks whenever he could fit them into his schedule. I was impressed from the first moment we met. We caught up each day for breakfast and sat together during the seminar sessions. We became 'instant' friends.

Harry had a daughter Stephanie to his ex-wife Yvonne. They had been divorced for over six years. Stephie was about to start high school. Harry had not remarried.

Harry and Stephie lived in Stanwell Park, south of Sydney, over an hour from me. Knowing he was (almost) in my city actually made me feel a little bit uncomfortable. This guy could be a real threat to my marriage. He was totally gorgeous!

Harry's work meant that he was away a lot travelling around Australia and New Zealand. Stephie stayed with her grandmother when Harry was away.

We shared stories of our lives, our successes and our disappointments.

Harry was charming, very charming indeed! But, I knew better... I knew what could happen, I knew that people could, would and **do** get hurt.

After the weekend was over, we shared a quick hug and then said our good-byes. We had exchanged phone numbers and email addresses so that we could keep in touch.

Diary Entry:

Sunday September 16th

What a great weekend. I met some great people and had a fab time. The seminar was interesting and I hope to catch up with people over the next few days. Can't wait to hear from Harry.

On 19 September 11:44 AM, "Harry" wrote:
Hi there,
It was great to meet you on the weekend. Thanks for
making my weekend in the Mountains so memorable. You
certainly know how to put a smile on my face, that's
for sure. You are a beautiful person Michelle, I
hope we get to spend more time together.
Look forward to catching up again real soon.
Harry

Just days after the seminar, I received my first email from Harry. He flattered me. I could certainly say the same about him. I hadn't stopped thinking about him since we had said good-bye. I kept re-playing our conversations we had over and over in my mind.

I remember him laughing at me because I got so paranoid about my hair getting wet in the rain and how he made fun of me when I drank my hot chocolate and got froth on the end of my nose.

I remember the hours sitting by the big log fireplace toasting marshmellows and burning way too many of them. I know that I drank too much hot chocolate that weekend that's for sure. Oh the memories...

I waited as long as I could then I emailed him back.

On 19 September 12:02 PM, "Michelle" wrote:
Hi you,
Good to hear from you. Yes I had a great weekend.
It was lovely to meet you. You have put a big smile
on my face too. I'm finding it tough to get back
into my work. Talk soon,
Michelle

On 19 September 12:20 PM, "Harry" wrote:
I'm glad you had a good weekend. I think we really clicked, did you feel that too? I know you're married but I would really like to be your friend. Would that be OK with you?

On 19 September 12:40 PM, "Michelle" wrote:
Yes we definitely clicked. I would love to be your friend. I haven't told Sean about you - for some reason it feels wrong. I know nothing happened between us on the weekend but I certainly felt a load of chemistry there.

On 19 September 12:56 PM, "Harry" wrote:
I know about the chemistry thing. It was buzzing my end too. I will try to remember you are a married woman, even though at times I wanted to... Oh, you probably didn't need to know that.

On 19 September 1:02 PM, "Michelle" wrote:
HARRY ! That's enough.

This was the start of the emails. Then came the phone calls and text messages. There was instant and continuous flirting. It all seemed like harmless fun but my intuition was talking to me again - very loudly!

Author's Learning:
When you are hiding a secret, you need to be sure to hide or delete of all the evidence. Being a detective in reverse was how I went about covering up my new found fun! Here's some of what I did.

Harry was listed in my mobile phone as 'Helen'. There were plenty of other Helen's in my life... so Sean would not be phased by another one. Emails were redirected to the 'junk' mail folder, so they would not be seen in the In Box. Text messages were deleted daily, even though they were from 'Helen'! A message saying "I think U R Sexy" from 'Helen' would raise alarm bells I believe.

My diary entries were always confidential in Sean's mind. We never read them together like Nick and I used to. I was pretty sure he wouldn't think to look there. If I was concerned, I would have found another book to write in or started an electronic diary.

Secrecy is a dangerous game - and I should have known better!

Diary Entry:

Thursday September 20th

What a great day. Harry called me. I feel so special. He really knows the right things to say. He wants to catch up next time he's in the city. Can't wait to see him. My stomach is telling me I shouldn't go. . . I know he will be trouble.

We knew we needed to see each other again. It was going to take a bit of organising with our busy schedules, work, children and so on.

'Will I go?'

'Should I go?'

'Is this the right thing to do?'

The innuendos from Harry were strong and very much to the point.

I knew it was time to start to hiding my diary. I didn't want Sean to find it. I wasn't ready to explain these feelings I was having for another man. It felt wrong but it also felt so nice.

We were in contact all the time. As the weeks passed we tried to see each other but our schedules just didn't match. There were many other activities going on and Harry was out of town so much.

On 3 October 8:34 AM, "Michelle" wrote:
Well, Harry,
You certainly do know how to push my buttons…
needless to say that Sean benefited greatly last
night from our 'fun' on the email yesterday… I was
about as horny as ever..

Therefore, I believe we should CANCEL all
arrangements to meet… I don't think I can trust
being around you. Or should I put it down to research
for a book???

On 3 October 8:53 AM "Harry" wrote:
Now I really needed to know about you riding your
husband hard last night... Tell me more... NOT
lol

I think research could be interesting. What would
the book be about?

On 3 October 9:40 AM, "Michelle" wrote:
I'm not sure exactly but I know there is a book in
me. Maybe I could write about the complexities
of relationships. Maybe love affairs. I have had
enough of those in my life. You know I've been
cheated on and I've also been the other woman,
maybe I should be the one to cheat for a change...
I could ask others about their experiences or just
do some personal research of my own. What do you
think?

On 3 October 10:23 AM "Harry" wrote:
I think you would be better writing from the first
person perspective....!!! Research it should be!

On 3 October 10:32 AM, "Michelle" wrote:
Ah, So you just want my body...

On 3 October 10:43 AM "Harry" wrote:
Ha ha ha...... No I enjoy your banter too

On 3 October 10:51 AM, "Michelle" wrote:
No????
No - you don't want my body
Or No - I want your body and enjoy your banter -
come on Harry you need to be more specific!!!

On 3 October 10:52 AM "Harry" wrote:
HA, Option 2...

Harry loved teasing and tempting me. He loved it. He was a born flirt and so was I. So it continued. Harry was in contact as often as he could. His days were busy so it was difficult for him to get away from work to call. Of course he couldn't contact me during the evenings as Sean and our children were around.

I was starting to feel guilty because of a show I had watched on TV. There were two females chatting about relationships. One (Jane) was madly in love with another woman's husband but she has so far resisted him sexually, although they had become close. Jane believes she's done the right thing and that she hasn't crossed the line.

The second woman (Martha) was married to a man who has been sending emails to another woman. Jane says that's okay for Martha's husband to do that as they haven't met or had any physical contact. Martha disagrees. She says the moment her husband shared an emotional feeling with the other woman that he had cheated on her.

That scene has been going over and over in my mind. It has been amazing to meet Harry. But is it wrong? It is in the eyes of Martha but I'm sure Jane would think it's fine... is it as simple as to what we believe to be right and wrong... My question was - what do I believe?

Diary Entry:

Monday October 8th

Harry called today and desperately wanting to know when we could catch up. After checking our busy schedules again it looks like he will be in the city the same time as I will be at a Women's conference later this month. We are so excited. Could it happen?

We are determined to make it happen. Two nights together just the two of us. Maybe that's too many... maybe not enough?

Our date was booked. Harry said he was very excited and nervous about meeting me. The countdown was on !!! There was no going back now.

After weeks of emails back and forth, it was now only days until I would see him again.

I felt incredibly nervous, excited, scared, exposed, strong and vulnerable all rolled up in one. I had so many concerns at the one time: 'I had better look my best. What should I wear? Better get my hair done. Got to look great. Should I get new lingerie?'

My head was full of questions, the loudest ones were;

'What was I doing?'

'What is the point of all this?'

'Why was I so nervous?'

We had two evenings planned. Our days were filled with work commitments but in the evening it was to be all about us. Romance was on the agenda for sure.

It was going to be our first meeting since the Mountains Seminar. Would this be our first time together? I had to get my story straight. My cover story to Sean was that I was attending a two day conference in Sydney. Rather than travel back and forth I would stay in the city and help with the 'behind the scenes' stuff'- that was pretty close to the truth!

Diary Entry:

Thursday October 25th

Well here I am in a beautiful Shangri-La hotel, ALONE in my room... there was a last minute issue with Harry's work and he is stuck over two hours out of town. Is this a co-incidence - are we really meant to do this? Maybe not.

I have spent the day networking and meeting fantastic women and a few men.

I'm tired, it's late but will wait by the phone and my computer to see what happens in the next hour. I'm sure he will check his email. I know he will. I hope he will.

I lie here thinking of the day's events. I can't wait til tomorrow night. It's sure to be a great night. I get butterflies just thinking about it. I'm glad this is not the only night we have planned.

I sent an email to Harry to see if he wanted to have outrageous phone sex tonight. I jumped in the shower and watched the laptop through the glass shower door. Would he reply. I didn't want to call, what if he was with work colleagues, what if he was asleep?

The hotel phone rang. My heart stopped. Panic. Did he even know where I was? Of course he did! I answered the phone, it was reception, wanting to check if I had a copy of my invoice. Phew. My heart started beating again.

My feelings were a scramble, I wanted it but I didn't want it. I thought it would be fun but I also knew Sean was alone in our bed. I knew my children were asleep in theirs. I asked myself over and over, "Why am I doing this? Why would I encourage this?" I desperately wanted to know the answer. The excitement of Harry was taking over the reality of my life.

Today, for the first time we had a few men at the women's networking event. I took the opportunity to ask some personal 'research' questions over dinner.

One of the men Brad, confirmed that men like to flirt. I knew that, who doesn't. So I ask the question; "Should it be something that we can continue to do throughout our lives, even when involved in a relationship? Why do we stop? Is it because society doesn't approve of those in a serious relationship or marriage to enjoy the art of flirting? Or do we really not trust ourselves about where it could take us?"

Apparently (confirmed by our other five dinner guests) the latter is true, we just don't trust ourselves.

Brad confirmed that he had cheated on his wife (apparently just once). He said a girl came up to him at a bar and said 'I want to rock your socks off'. Brad was shocked by her forwardness but within seconds had accepted her offer.

Brad went on to confirm for me that alcohol doesn't have to be involved when a man cheats. Given the right situation most men will cheat, "It's just for sex", he said. "As long as the emotional feelings are not there - then it's okay". I glared at him and questioned, "It's OKAY?" as if he had accepted to play a round of tennis.

I asked Brad if he would ever tell his wife – apparently not. I let him know that no matter how hard he tried to hide it, women have amazing intuition and even though he hadn't told her, I'm sure she knew and she knows!

He looked at me, questioning my comment. I went on to tell him how amazing women are and that his wife would have felt the change in him, however slight it might have be.

So he asked, "If they know, then why do women stay?"

My answer, came in an Author's Learning:
"Many women deny 'what' they know and the fact 'that' they know. Some prefer to keep what they have rather than lose it. They stay and have some kind of relationship, rather than be left without a partner in their lives. Some feel guilty that they are the ones at fault for their partner straying."

Brad goes on to confirm that most men that cheat will keep their secret to themselves, some may share with other guys to prove their manhood.

Ding! 'email received'. I hoped the email was from Harry. But it was just the Woolworths' newsletter of weekly specials.

Anxious about tomorrow night, I attempted to get some sleep.

Diary Entry:

Sunday October 28th

Well tonight was sensational. It all happened way too fast. Time went way too quickly. We had dinner at a Thai Restaurant. We ate quickly. We knew where this was going. We just had to get there. Back at my hotel it was really special. Harry made love to me. It *was amazing! My emotions are all over the place. WRONG vs RIGHT . . It is difficult to keep my thoughts under control but it's easy to be with Harry. He makes everything so beautiful.*

The sex was great, our connection was incredible. I need to spend more time with him. My only concern now is my life.... Sean, the kids... How do I go on? How do I go back to them? How do I cover this up.

Our night was planned to start at 6:30pm. Harry met me in the bar of the Shangri-La Hotel. I was the one deceiving my husband.

My stomach had never churned so much or felt so much anticipation.

I got to the bar early - I wanted to be the one waiting for him - not him waiting for me. Not sure why, I just needed to be there first.

He arrived on time and he came towards me at the bar.

I said "Hello". He didn't speak.

His hand softly touched my face. His thumb slightly brushed my bottom lip. My lip was pulled down, he moved closer. His breath was warm and the thought of his lips on mine, shuddered my body.

The seconds ticked by, it seemed like forever. Slowly his lips approached mine, they were soft and ready to devour me. I felt guilty, his kiss was amazing, I wanted to be with him but at the same time I didn't.

As the kiss ended, he softly whispered 'Hellooooo' and I felt my knees weaken.

I said "Hello, nice to see you again," I wanted another kiss.

We sat, ate dinner and talked for ages as the anticipation between us grew. We discussed how we needed to organise to spend more time together.

Dinner was lovely but we skipped dessert. We could have gone back to the bar in the hotel but we both knew where we wanted to go. Our phone calls and emails had prepared us for that. There was chemistry and there was a very, very strong desire.

As we approached the hotel room, I felt completely out of control. Knowing it was wrong, knowing that it could end badly I went anyway.

Harry put the key in the door and then held the door open as we went in. The door closed behind us, he pushed me against the door and kissed me again. That kiss was even better than the first!

We stood against the door for a while, he kissed me again and again. His kisses were warm and gentle. He kissed my face, my neck and my ears. I was totally under his spell.

Being with Harry was sensual, caring and very passionate.

Our bodies were not as fit and youthful as we both would have liked them to be but the physical body didn't matter. There was no stopping this, it was too late. I was so engrossed in the moment to realise or think about what I was doing to those I loved.

We made love to each other, his hands were gentle and his touch was tender but Harry understood that this was not easy for me.

Being with Harry meant cheating on Sean and on my two beautiful children.

Harry knew I needed some time. My mind was racing. It didn't take long after many sensual kisses I gave into the moment, gave into temptation. It was easier than I thought it would be. Instantly, I had an appreciation of what Dan and Nick had experienced.

To be in a situation where you feel you have to go with the flow - felt good even if it was wrong.

I was enjoying myself with Harry but I knew what was happening was a big betrayal in Sean's eyes. How would I hide the huge smile from my face? What would he do if he found out? I tried to block out those thoughts!

So began my new "double life".

As I lay absorbed in Harry's arms my mind finally stopped racing. It was just so wonderful to be with Harry, lying quietly together.

Harry had to leave shortly afterwards. He had to drive all the way home that night. It was difficult to let him go but I knew there would definitely be a next time.

After our sad goodbye, I laid alone in the huge bed, thinking. Happy about what had happened. Saddened by what had happened. It was the weirdest feeling, knowing that you can spend time with someone that makes you feel alive and excited and at the same time knowing that my husband was not aware of any of it.

I felt like I could split my body into pieces, happy, sad, sorry. This was the start of many new secrets. Sean's often voiced comment echoed in my ears, 'If you ever have an affair, don't bother coming back".

I needed sleep. I didn't think that was going to be possible? The bed suddenly felt very empty.

As I travelled home the next morning, reality and fear accompanied me for what happened the previous night.

At least I was able to say it was a successful event.

Sean was a great guy. I couldn't do without him. Sean still excited me, just differently to how Harry did. I knew Sean, we'd been together for almost a decade but Harry was fresh, new, exciting and sparked a real interest in me.

Author's Learnings:

By now, I know what is required if you want to be somewhere, with someone and you don't want your partner knowing. There has to be planning, secrets and lots of lies! The cover up story mixed with a bit of truth.

I had been on the receiving end of a cheating husband. I saw and felt the signs.

I had been the other woman. I heard the lies that were told. I experienced how the plans were made and how deceitful you have to be over and over again to cover the truth from being exposed.

So you are asking - How could I do this? Looking back I can clearly see that Harry was the missing piece of my puzzle. Question was, could I find that within my marriage or within myself?

After the children came along Sean and I didn't really have much of a sex life but that's normal. Everyone tells you that 'it takes a while to get your libido back.' Sean understood and joked about it all the time. "Sex once a month!" he would tell our friends... I don't remember it ever being that bad but he got great mileage out of it. I was now in such a different sexual place to where I was pre-children.

As the children got older, I started enjoying our sexual relationship more and more. As the children became more independent and I was finally on the improve in the 'zing' department, our sex life started getting a whole lot better.

The excitement with Harry definitely helped my relationship with Sean. I felt more fulfilled and more of a loving person to be around.

I guess you could say that Harry completed me.

Diary Entry:

Tuesday November 6th

I emailed Harry today to see when next we could get together ?

He bowled me over when he told me his ex-wife Yvonne died last night. Everything is upside down and his daughter Stephie is totally shattered. I can't believe it. I feel just awful for him and his daughter.

I gave him my condolences and offered to help if he needed it. What more do you say in these situations?

I felt sad. Sad for Harry and for his daughter. Yvonne had been suffering breast cancer for the past eleven years. After being in remission for over four years, it had returned and attacked her body again.

Harry and Stephie flew to Hobart to attend Yvonne's funeral. They were gone for days. I missed the communication between us. I was constantly thinking of Harry and what he and his daughter were going through. I wondered how Harry would be feeling. A large part of his life had ended.

Diary Entry:

Wednesday November 14th

He's back! It feels weird after all he and Stephie have been thru that he's so keen to see me again. It was nice to hear from him. He's calling me tomorrow, when he's going to have more time to talk... I can't believe how much I missed him.

I received an email from Harry - they were back. It was good to hear from him and know everything was kind-of okay. We planned to speak the following day and have a chat about their trip.

Just the excitement of talking to Harry the next day meant that I didn't sleep very well. I tossed and turned most of the night. I was on my own for half the night until Sean arrived home from a night out with the boys. He found me naked in our bed - he knew I was horny again.

It was so good to know I was getting my 'zing' back. My question was "is it 'me' getting my zing back or is it Harry giving me my zing back?". Either way, Sean was definitely benefiting and not complaining.

Harry hated to hear that I was having great sex with Sean but I felt a little cheeky when I shared this with him. I just had to rub it in a little more. I couldn't resist emphasizing how great I was and that he was missing out!

It was very dangerous flirting.

Diary Entry:

Thursday November 15th

It was great to talk to Harry today, he definitely does it for me. Whatever 'it' is... We talked about Stephie and how she was coping with the loss of her Mum. We planned our next date. It's going to be nice to see him again. Harry is doing all the planning. Yippee!

Morning finally arrived and I was really looking forward to talking to Harry. After getting the children off to school, I left him a message. Harry returned my call. It was great to hear him say 'Hellooooo'. We talked about his trip to Hobart. He was relieved that Stephie had been with him at the time and that she wasn't living with Yvonne in Hobart. Harry referred to it as a chapter of his life finally being closed. Now they could both move on with their lives.

Harry confirmed that everything was planned for our dinner. I knew I would cancel anything to see him. I would make it happen. As it was only a few weeks before Christmas it would be easy to make excuses and sneak away. I hated lying to Sean but my desire to be with Harry was strong.

Harry was a big part of my life now, I had accepted that. He consumed my thoughts. If I'd been away from home for a while, I would come back and the first thing I would do when I walked in the door was check my email. Had he been in contact? I needed to get myself together and achieve getting some work done. It was totally obsessive. The excitement of it all was wonderful. The thought of getting caught was always on my mind. The tricks I had learnt to cover things up had definitely kicked in and were working at full speed.

Diary Entry:

Tuesday December 4th

Harry called to cancel our dinner plans. I'm feeling very low. It was our only chance to see each other before the New Year, I am sad!

Harry had to take an unexpected trip to Canberra. No chance to be together before Christmas or the New Year. I was so disappointed. It was difficult for him to get away during the school holidays and with his work. So it was going to be a while until we could be together again. We talked constantly on the phone and emails continued to fly between us.

On 24/December 11:34 AM, "Harry" wrote:
Merry Christmas Special Lady,
I hope your Christmas is filled with memories both great and small, may Santa bring you all that you wish for (hope that includes me)... See you soon... Love me (Harry) xxx

On 24/December 1:42 PM, "Michelle" wrote:
Merry Christmas Special Man,
Ditto to you too. Santa might not visit as I haven't been very good lately (ha ha). I hope you and Stephie have a lovely holiday together. Look forward to talking again soon, love me x

Diary Entry:

Christmas Day December 25th

Day spent with family. It was good to have a laugh. The kids had a great day. Santa was good to them. It's great to see everyone so happy.

Weeks passed, we had celebrated birthdays, Christmas and New Year. Another year over, how quickly the years were flying by.

Over Christmas and New Year Harry purchased a property in the country. Stephie and Harry had moved in over the Summer holidays. Their new home was out of mobile phone range. I received the occasional email from an Internet Cafe just keeping me in the loop saying they still hadn't been connected to the phone or internet.

More and more days passed. I missed our constant banter on the email, I missed his voice at the other end of the phone. Was he missing me? The remote access was doing my head in. I was feeling less and less confident about my relationship with Harry. I should have been concentrating on my relationship with Sean but it was Harry that was always on my mind.

I stayed busy with school holiday activities with the children and we went to the beach as often as we could. All the time I was thinking :

'What was he up to?'

'Where was he?'

'Why has he not contacted me?'

It was tough getting through the days, the weeks. I was missing him.

I was not enjoying the lack of contact. I was feeling very lonely. It bought back feelings and memories of years ago with Nick and those times when we could not make contact.

More weeks passed. I still heard nothing.

Maybe that was it. Maybe it was over.

Maybe it was all too difficult.

Maybe it was for the best!

Diary Entry:

Wednesday January 23rd

I heard from Harry today. It was so nice to hear his voice. Finally he's settled into his new place and the internet and landline have been connected. It feels great to have contact with him again. We chatted for ages, it so good – He's back!

After almost a month of being off the air, it was all back on. Emails resumed about how much we had been missing each other. How much we wanted to be together again. It was tough to cover the smile that stretched from one side of my face to the other. I was instantly feeling special again. My feeling of loneliness just vanished.

Harry was going to be in Brisbane the entire month of February so I found a 'business' opportunity to go to Brisbane for some training. I deliberated over the decision to go for a few days. I knew I had to make it look to Sean like I didn't really care if I went or not. Finally I said I would go and visit some clients and make it a business trip. Sean said it made good sense and if I organised the children before and after school then I should go.

So the plan was set. Harry and I in the same city at the same time. It was thrilling and such an uplifting feeling. Could I get away with it?

With my mind wandering, I found it difficult to concentrate. I was not achieving much work at all. I became very thankful that I have understanding clients.

Harry too was eager about our trip. We would be spending an entire day (and night) together. We were both so excited.

Diary Entry:

Monday January 28th

Days are going way too slow right now. The nerves are already setting in. I am feeling torn between right and wrong. Too many more sleeps.

Diary Entry:

Friday February 1st

Wow. Sean and I had a great big chat about affairs today and why people have them. His view is if you are going to cheat, then end it first with your partner. OK for him to say!

Sean and I had been talking about 'affairs'. There seems to be a lot of that subject going around. It's on the television, it's being talked about on the radio. They were even promoting a website that allows people who want to cheat to meet. This started an in-depth conversation with Sean. His point of view was simple. If you are going to cheat - end it first with the partner you have. Ouch. That hurt.

Again, I asked myself, 'What was I doing?' "Why was I doing this?"

I couldn't end it with Sean.

Our relationship was good. We had certainly had wonderful years together and our children were a very good reason to stay together and work it all out. I knew they didn't deserve to go through a separation and I wasn't ready for that either.

So WHY? Why was I cheating? What was it that made it appropriate and acceptable in my mind?

The only thing I could grasp at this point was that it was 'fun'. The thrill of the chase, the sneaking around, the excitement and anticipation of it all. I hadn't planned to have an affair. I certainly didn't want to jeopardise my marriage.

The affair made me feel special like when I was in love with Nick. That feeling had returned and I liked it.

Yes, I was older now and certainly knew better but not enough to change anything.

Diary Entries:

Tuesday February 5th

Only two more sleeps to go. I am nervous. What if Sean realises what's going on... I'm looking forward to being in Harry's arms again, being held tight and feeling loved and wanted.

Thursday February 7th

I arrived in Brisbane today and attended a business meeting. I spoke with Harry and all is planned for tomorrow. It's been a while since we were together. I'm staying overnight and Harry will be driving me to the airport on Saturday morning in his hire car. Wow... this will be the longest time we have ever spent together alone. Not sure what else to write now, I'm anxious that's for sure... and a bit scared!

Friday February 8th

I didn't sleep well last night. The thought of today being our day together was just too much to justify much sleep. Harry arrived after his appointment. He met me at a little cafe overlooking the city. He walked in and just smiled, he looked so handsome. The entire afternoon was planned by Harry and we had such a great time. He definitely made it special. My favourite bit was the ferris wheel ride, followed by a wonderful night in his arms.

Harry arrived just after midday. He strolled into Bella Cafe, with his adorable smile. Intention was in his eyes. I got up to give him a hug. He gave me a quick kiss and sat down next to me in the booth. With his arms around me, he kissed me passionately. I had missed him so much more than I realised. It felt so comfortable being with him.

We had a great table overlooking the river and Brisbane city. We ordered our meals and chatted through lunch. It was nice to know we had the entire afternoon and evening together without a worry in the world.

After lunch we drove down the road and had heaps of fun at a local family fair. We laughed and played all afternoon, enjoying kisses and cuddles wherever we could. Harry knew how to have a good time and it make me feel special.

We raced each other down the giant slides, crashed the bumper cars and squashed up against one another on the roller coaster. I gave up on the shooting target games, I had no hope against 'the professional archer'. Well that's what he called himself - all very proud!

Then we went on the ferris wheel. This was my favourite. We didn't see much of the scenery. It was wonderful sitting on top of the world being kissed by an amazing man - my Harry.

We left the fair and went back to the hotel, we had some Japanese noodles for dinner and then straight to our hotel room.

Calling home was quite a different story. Having Harry in the room while I spoke to Sean and the children was the toughest part. I kept telling myself 'as long as there weren't too many lies'. I thought I would be okay. Sean had so much trust in me that he didn't even ask where I was or what I had been doing. Phew! I had got away with it for now.

Hearing my children's voices was crushing. Knowing I had just spent a wonderful afternoon with a man they didn't even know, felt really horrible.

Having Harry see the "Mum" side of me was important. He appreciated that it was who I was and that being on this side of the triangle was no fun for me at all. Harry could see the concern and discomfort on my face. We had fun, but now it didn't feel right.

When I was with Harry, it was like I was someone else. Not a mum, not a wife, not a daughter, not someone's friend - just me. An escape from my life, from my daily existence. It took a while until I softened into him again... reality had revealed itself.

Harry and I fit together so well, his body enveloped mine, so much that we could have stayed in that hotel room forever. The tenderness and caring was beautiful. The sex wasn't bad either! Harry certainly knew how to make me feel amazing. It's true as you get older the sex changes, it was so sensual.

Harry always made me laugh, he'd say things like, "Stop that frowning or you'll get wrinkly" or "You're the sweet icing on my world of boring cake".

He caressed and touched me so passionately that I wanted to cry. It was so lovely being with Harry. The passion was intense. 'My' passion was more intense. My mind wasn't crazy like the first time we were together. I was much more relaxed and comfortable. It was afterwards that my mind started to race again with constant questions of why.

"Why was I doing it? It was great. It was wrong". The questions tumbled over and over. It was not easy to know what to do, but I realised that it was my decision to make.

Having Harry share my bed was a treat. If only I could go to sleep. Snuggled up under Harry's arm feeling protected and safe was amazing. It was the one thing I didn't get to do with Sean, but I didnt' sleep

Diary Entry:

Saturday February 9th

It was tough to leave Harry this morning. We woke early and enjoyed being close to each other again. The drive to the airport was silent. A comfortable sad quiet. There wasn't much that needed to be said. I knew I had to go home again. Sean and the kids met me at the airport, the kids calling out to me at the top of their voices as I *came down the escalator. I nearly cried. I'm finding it hard now. My thoughts are of yesterday and what I to do.*

Waking up next to Harry was really special. I felt tired after I had tossed and turned all night. At around 4am, I got up and sat on the edge of the bed. I'd had enough of trying to sleep. Next thing I knew I was being pulled in close, snuggled with my forehead being stroked. He cared for me so much. Our love was growing and I felt I was unable to stop it.

In the morning Harry gave me an early Valentine's Day present, a cute little teddy bear with 'I love you' written on his tummy. My first thought was 'How was I going to get that one home?'

We knew we wouldn't be together for Valentine's Day, so we had morning sex followed by yummy room service breakfast in bed.

I didn't feel guilty like I thought I would. I wanted to be there, I really did. I wasn't' feeling bad or wrong. Things felt nice. I liked waking up and spending time with Harry.

I was feeling okay until I was at the airport alone waiting for my flight. It finally hit me that I was going home to face my family.

I got off the plane in Sydney and walked down to get my bags, my children were at the bottom of the escalator yelling out 'Mummy'. They were so excited to see me. People were looking up at me, I felt awful. I held back the tears as they welled in my eyes. Sean came over and gave me a kiss and cuddle. The kids' excitement to have me back after such a short time was gorgeous.

Reality hit me hard. The children - my children - how could I do this to them? How could I do this to us?

The realisation of what I would or could lose was very strong. My life wasn't bad. Sean would never forgive me - no way.

Back home and back to the emails again. First thing Monday morning I wrote to Harry with my news.

On 11 February 7:34 AM, "Michelle" wrote:
Well it's very true… I'm missing my Harry already. Thank you for a wonderful time.
Yesterday was tough… not enough sleep, being hurled back into my life. The show was ok, coffee afterwards with friends was nice, kids running everywhere – not so nice. Dinner with 'family' was strange. Too tired to care…

I have had a great night sleep… I went to sleep with my thoughts of our night together. xx

In saying that, I want you to know that I had a real breakthrough lying next to you in the darkness of the night. It feels amazing. I know my <u>why</u>. You bring something to my life that is missing and something I've been longing for.

Now I know what it is and why I'm so attracted to you. You are someone who cares for me… the way you covered me up with blankets and surrounded me with (can I say) love, was so beautiful. You understand me. Without a word being spoken… I do all the caring in my house. I just need someone to care for me. I know Sean loves me but what I'm talking about is more than just love. I know I am a strong, confident and an independent woman but I need strong arms around me sometimes too.

Now, how do I move forward? I just want to go back and be snuggled up under your arm with your body beside me…

Saying goodbye and letting you go of you at the airport was the hardest thing.

Oh and I feel annoyed that I have lost the ability to fall asleep with someone touching me and holding me.

Today I'm home alone with the kids… my thoughts will be on our time together and hopefully I'll find the energy to go and hang the washing and get some work done…

I know we will talk soon but I just felt I needed to share this with you – you know me – always the writer… I will thank the universe every day for allowing me to meet you. XXX

On 11 February 11:42 AM, "Harry" wrote:
That's fantastic news that you have figured out your 'why'. I know that has been on your mind for some time now.
I'm annoyed too that you didn't sleep when we were together, I loved holding you close to me.
I missed you after dropping you at the airport. It was a lonely drive back into the city.

```
I miss you so much.  I do care for you - you are a
special lady and I'm glad I can give you that piece
of the puzzle that is missing for you.
X Your Harry
```

Returning home after being with Harry was tough. Feelings of sadness overwhelmed me at times. I didn't know what I wanted anymore. Could I stay in my life, now that I understood why? Was it a strong enough reason to leave? How could I figure out what I wanted and needed? What should I do next? Should I make my decisions for me, or for my family?

The following days were difficult. I went through many emotions. Sean put it down to the fact that I didn't sleep well in another bed and it was 'that' time of the month. The combination meant I was a bit unbearable to say the least.

The children drove me mad, it was hard to concentrate on my work. On the days that Harry didn't phone, text or email me - I was lost. I had come to rely on his contact. To feel alive. To feel life. To feel whole!

There I was back on the roller coaster again! I couldn't believe that I had allowed myself back on that crazy ride.

Diary Entry:

Thursday February 14th

Valentine's Day today, it came and went. Harry's teddy bear sits on top of my computer. Sean doesn't even notice it. Sean bought me home a bunch of flowers from the Servo. It's the thought that counts!

I had constant feelings and memories of Harry. I needed to focus more on my work and my life with my family. How do I do that? Sometimes I felt very lonely and sad. I would like to feel alive. I asked myself, "Is this my lot? Is there more in store for my life?"

I waited for Harry to call me.

Every time I received an email or a text message it would cheer me up for hours. Hearing him call me 'gorgeous' or 'sweetie' made my day.

Diary Entry:

Tuesday February 19th

Today I struggled to get anything done. After dropping the kids at school I came home and had a coffee and achieved absolutely nothing. Work needs to be done but I just can't do it. Sean is being supportive and thinks I just need sleep. How do I sort this out in my own head. Oh I wish I had someone to talk to.

My break through to my 'WHY' was important. I decided I needed to discuss my needs with Sean but my desire to be with Harry hadn't stopped.

Diary Entry:

Wednesday February 20th

I loved meeting with Harry for a 'lunch' date. It was fun just being close. No time for more than some food and a cuddle or two.

Harry and I met in Balmain for a quick lunch. He was in town and I made the trip over to be with him. We went to my old favourite pub, the Dry Dock Hotel and enjoyed a few hours together before I had to pick up the kids from school. We would have loved to have stayed longer, but neither of us could afford the extra time.

Harry could see I was happy to see him but that my brain was struggling being there with him. I didn't like being the cheating wife that I had become.

Diary Entry:

Friday February 22nd

Sean and I had a talk tonight about being closer - physically. Sean has never been able to sleep with me in his arms. We tried it again tonight but no luck. He says he wants to work on it, he sort of understands...

Sean and I talked about me being a control freak and how most of the decisions in our lives were made by me. He says it's easier to give in and let me decide - that way I am happy and he gets sex. He says all the guys do the same. That made me feel Great!

I needed him to be the 'man' of the house. To care for me. To protect me. I'm the one that looks after everyone else but I needed that for me too.

Sean and I tried to lay close and cuddle that night. We tried to cuddle while falling asleep. It's impossible. Sean can't do it. He can't go to sleep holding me or even being touched by me. My need for this gets stronger. Sean agreed to keep trying.

Diary Entry:

Tuesday February 26th

I received a text message that said 'Hi gorgeous, How r u? TOU' It always feels great to hear from Harry. I called him back and we chatted for ages.

Even the smallest contact made my days go by so much faster. I had to text back to ask what 'TOU' was... it's 'Thinking of You!' Oh, so sweet...

Diary Entry:

Thursday February 28th

I'm on top of the world! Harry and I have booked our next 'meeting'. Harry's response - "AWESOME". Can't wait to see him and be in his arms again. My spirit is inspired yet again.

I initiated our next date with Harry. I needed to see him so once a date was set I instantly felt happier knowing I would be with Harry soon. I only had to wait two more weeks.

My brain continues to work overtime. I kept thinking to myself, 'How can this go on?' ... deep down I don't think it can.

Diary Entry:

Saturday March 1st

I've decided it's time to make a decision. I can't keep deceiving Sean like this. I'm not enjoying the feeling I get when I look at him. I know I have to end it with Harry and fix it with Sean.

I cried at my children's special school parade. I was so proud of them. I had tears rolling down my face. Other parents must have thought there was something wrong with me. I was a total mess.

It was now hitting me hard. I was cheating and it was not right. Sean was a wonderful, kind man and a great father. We had lovely children and a nice life. Yes, Harry was exciting but where was this leading? It wasn't fair on the children, on Sean or on me!

I had to build some courage and stand strong. Stop giving in to Harry's voice and his smile. Listen to my intuition.

I wasn't going to leave Sean, I knew that after all my Temptation Triangle moments! Dan left. Nick stayed. I was going to do as Nick did and stay. My intuition was strong. The more I thought about it, the more convinced I became that my decision to stay was the right one.

The faces of our beautiful children were etched in my mind. They deserved a home filled with love and care. I owed it to them when I brought them into the world. Life with Sean wasn't at all horrible and I was so sure we could work on it.

I had to tell Harry.

Diary Entry:

Monday March 3rd

Harry's in Western Australia til Wednesday. I tried to call him first thing this morning but went through to his message service. I waited to hear from him for hours coz of the time difference... He finally called me at lunchtime and I shared my decision. He wasn't happy. He doesn't want to give me up. Oh no! My period still hasn't arrived and my breasts are killing me. Here's hoping it arrives tonight...

Diary Entry:

Tuesday March 4th

I'm feeling yuck today... not good. I think this decision making stress is getting to me. Hope I feel better soon.

The next few days I received may emails and text messages. Harry would not accept my decision to stop seeing him. He told me he loves me. He'd never said that out loud before. Was he just saying that to try and keep me in his life? I was confused.

I wasn't enjoying it anymore.

Diary Entry:

Thursday March 6th

OMG... I am stunned and afraid of what had happened today... Harry arriving without telling me. Stephie was lovely, a real sweetie. Our girls would be great friends, I just know it. I need to talk to

Sean. I need to make him aware of what happened here today... I'm worried about his reaction. He will be crushed and will put on a brave face but I don't think it will be good.

What now? All I have to do is roll over and spill the beans... wish me luck... Oh, I wish this diary could talk back to me... some advice right now would be great!

It was just after lunch when I heard a knock at the front door. I got up from my desk and answered it.

Harry was standing there. "Hellllllloooo" he said. "Hello" I replied, quite stunned that he was standing in my doorway. Why was he there? Why hadn't he told me he was coming?

I looked into his eyes for answers to my unasked questions.

"I want you to come and meet someone" he instructed as he looked back down the driveway. There must be someone in the car, my mind raced.

"Who's that?" I asked. "I want you to meet *your* step-daughter," he said. I was stunned, WHAT?

Had he gone mad, I didn't have a step-daughter, what was he talking about? Oh!

"Stephie saw how sad I was about your decision" he started, "and she convinced me that I should follow my dreams and my dream is to have YOU in our lives!"

I followed him down the driveway, like I was walking in slow motion. I was speechless, my heart raced. I had never seen him like this before, it looked like he was on a mission and was doing all he could to make it happen. I didn't know what to say. So many things ran through my mind. What should I do? What did all this mean for everyone involved?

There was Stephie sitting in the car with a big smile right the way across her beautiful face. I knew it was her. She resembled her father quite remarkably. She obviously knew of his plan.

"Hi there" she said, "nice to finally meet you!"

"Nice to meet you too. Your Dad has told me so much about you" I replied.

"Not as much as he's told me about you," she giggled.

I looked back at Harry, he was a little embarrassed that we were talking about him. He was calm and extremely happy. He looked very proud of the three of us laughing together.

All I could think about was - there is another family. My family. My children. My husband!

Harry and Stephie came inside and stayed for a cup of tea (or two). It was nice to get to know Stephie, she had been through so much for a young lady.

It was very strange having them in my home.

"So how do you feel about all this?" Harry asked with his mug covering his mouth.

"I'm very angry!" I replied. "You could have let me know you were dropping in today, I would have done my hair" trying to make light of the situation and shift my awkwardness.

He knew that I was uncomfortable. It would have been so different if he had come alone. At least this way I could be strong.

There wasn't much time. I had to do school pick up in an hour. We talked and laughed and as the time went by Harry made his intentions clear.

"I want you - I love you and I need you in my life, in our lives." He went on. "I know it will take some time, I am happy to wait - as long as it takes".

He was happy that he had come to say what he wanted to say. I, however, was in absolute shock!

He kissed me on the forehead and said "I'll see you soon, very soon!" Harry and Stephie left as I went to pick up my children from school.

Things had officially got out of control. It had become way too serious. I had to take a stand. I had to decide and not allow anyone to sway my choice. It was very difficult. I loved Harry. I loved Sean.

Harry had stood up and was ready to take from life the things that he wanted. Was it that easy? This is what I had waited for and wanted from Nick all those years ago. Why was this happening now?

I went and found my old sapphire ring and wore it as a reminder that I needed to make good decisions for me.

After making my diary entry that night, I put my diary in the top drawer of my bedside table and rolled over to 'share all' with Sean. I hadn't really stopped to think *how* I would do that exactly but knew that I had to be honest and let Sean know what was going on.

I explained that I had a visitor today. He was not phased at first. Then I shared that my visitor was a man 'wanting me to be with him'. Sean thought I was joking and that it was all just a bit of fun. He laughed and said "Go for it" then he looked into my eyes and realised I wasn't trying to be funny.

Now that I had his attention I could provide him with more information?

"Back in September, when I went to the Mountains, I met a man called Harry..."

I stopped, wanting to catch my breath and I realised what I had just said. The words echoed in my ears. Sean was shocked.

Then came his first question. "So what did you say?"

Sean was now looking concerned.

"I didn't give him an answer! I couldn't". Silence fell on the room.

"So does that mean you want to leave?" Sean continued his questioning.

I continued to tell Sean all about my relationship with Harry. I told him I wanted to stay with him and be a good mum to our children. "I want to grow old together, just like we planned", I tried to assure him.

Sean and I talked for hours. It was difficult to share Harry with him. It had been my secret for months but I knew I had to confess it all if we were to move on. Sean was hurt, very hurt. It brought back memories for me of when I found out about Dan and Kristina.

But I had to do the right thing for me, the right thing for Sean and for the children.

I didn't want to leave Sean and the children but how would I know if he could ever forgive me, if he would ever trust me again.

Sean was so angry. At one point he got up and left the room. He needed space and I didn't blame him for that. It definitely had all come as a shock.

He kept asking the same question. WHY?

I could only reassure him it wasn't planned and not something I went searching for. I tried to explain about my need to have someone look after me. Sean tried to understand however I'm sure in his mind that wasn't a valid reason.

It was late and we both needed sleep. I closed my eyes and laid there in the dark for what seemed like an eternity. What had I done?

Diary Entry:

Friday March 7th

Feeling extremely exhausted and sick today. Harry called – I told him that Sean knows. He was shocked. Harry was concerned for me and what I went thru last night. I re-confirmed with him that it had to be over for us and I was working it out with Sean.

The next day was exhausting. My mind churned over all the things from the previous days conversations. Harry loved me, Sean was disappointed in me. Sean was trying to understand. Harry thought I should have more time to think.

I had made my decision. It had to be over with Harry and I needed time to work it out for me. I had to find myself again and build my strength and love for me.

Sean got home from work late. I think he stayed at work as long as he could so he didn't have to face me. We tiptoed around each other until the children went to bed. His first question was "So, did you see Harry today?" "No" I answered, "but I did talk to him". "I told him that you know everything."

"Does he still want you?" Sean asked.

"Yes" I replied.

"Maybe you should go be with him then" Sean said.

"I don't want to". "I want to stay here with you and our family", I blurted out trying to stop my tears.

"Do you want me to go?" I asked.

There was no answer.

So began another difficult night of talking and crying. Sean started to feel like he was to blame. I tried to explain that it was not his fault.

In the morning, I felt like it just might be okay.

Diary Entry:

Saturday March 8th

Today I found out I'm pregnant. I took two tests... then I went to the doctor... Why... Why ???

I knew the baby was Harry's. I was sure of it. It was our pre-Valentine's Day morning sex when we didn't use any protection.

This was not how it was meant to be. I had to think things through quickly. I couldn't tell anyone. I just couldn't. I felt ashamed and guilty for allowing things to get this far.

I could terminate my pregnancy. I *could* tell Harry. I *should* tell Sean.

I had no idea what I was going to do???

Harry was right, I did need time to think...

Moral of Side 3:

This is a difficult side of the Triangle. On this side I had all the control, I got to make the decisions. My advice is if you have any issues or concerns in your relationships that you need to openly communicate and be truthful to those you love.

If you believe your relationship is worth saving, it can be saved. Forgiveness is possible.

If you do cheat - know the risks. They are very high. Knowing the tricks so you can cover them up is important... and accept that there will be lies, many, many lies. Know also, that you may get caught and you may hurt others.

Very few people get to have their cake and eat it too...

What happened next:

Sean & I sought months and months of counselling. We worked through my infidelity and slowly he was able to restore his trust in me. It took a long time to get our marriage back on track. In writing our story I fell in love with him all over again. I have stayed strong and committed to my husband and to our children.

Harry is the father of my 15 week old miscarried child. We secretly talk every now and then. He and Stephie still live on their property. Harry has a lovely new lady in his life.

Follow your Dream

Follow your dream
Wherever it leads,
Don't be distracted
By less worthy needs.
Shelter it, nourish it,
Help it to grow,
Follow your dream
Wherever it goes.

Follow your dream
Pursue it with haste,
Life is too fleeting
Too precious to waste.
Be faithful, be loyal,
Then all your life through
The dreams that you follow
Will keep coming true.

Author Unknown

May this be true for you.

Remember...

Life is not a dress rehearsal.

Moral of the Book:

We know strength comes from going through the darkest times. You find courage, determination, strength and many other characteristics that mould the person you are destined to be.

As women, knowing our intuition is the most powerful tool we have. Listen to it. Recognise it. It's your brain and body's way of telling you what you need to know. So tune in.

Each side of The Temptation Triangle is difficult. No side is easier than the other. Hurt and pain are awful experiences to have in your life. To avoid this, I think Sean's advice is the best - end your current relationship first before starting a new one.

Also know that someone always ends up getting hurt. It could be you. There can not be three 'knowing' people in a triangle relationship where it is fair and equal to all people involved.

If you need help - get help. There is no shame in asking for help. No matter what difficult relationship circumstances you may have, there is always someone to turn to. Someone who has been in your shoes before. Someone to give you advise and comfort. Someone to listen. You don't need to go through the dark times alone. Help is available!

You might like to try the exercise over the page that will ask you some challenging questions about your relationship.

www.TheTemptationTriangle.com

Author's Learnings:

Here are a few things I learnt when writing this book:

I learnt that the pain I have experienced in my life still travels with me.

I learnt to appreciate that all relationships are complex, whether it is with my husband, children, parents, family, friends or colleagues.

I learnt that there is temptation out there everyday, whether it be another person, a job or a sport that takes you away (both in time and emotion) from those you love.

I learnt that my diary did not have as much importance in my life when I had someone wonderful to share my thoughts and feelings with.

I learnt that relationships need constant work and open communication if they are going to grow and be positive for all involved.

I learnt that all three sides of The Temptation Triangle have their difficulties.

I learnt never say *Never*!

I learnt that I need to value and treasure my friends, family and my husband every day for their understanding and acceptance of me in their lives.

I hope that in sharing this you will understand more of the complexities of The Temptation Triangle.

Affair Survival Tools

The following pages are your personal psychology session approved by Psychologist, Dr Julie Ford. Our aim is to give you some questions that really make you think about what you want out of your relationships and your life.

Songs too are powerful. I have included the words of songs that helped me thru my toughest times. Even songs that are targeted to others, sing them with conviction and voice, it will make you feel great.

And of course remember to write. From page 158 you will see space for your diary entry as well as space to list all that you are grateful for. I encourage you to give it a try. Even if you start out small, for example; I am grateful for the sun that rises every morning, for the air I breath, for the great family and friends I have around me... Be grateful and great things will come to you.

So when you fill up the rest of the pages in this book, go and buy a Journal that you just love. Treasure it and enjoy, the power of writing.

Here's to your future.

Personal Psychology Session

Are you being cheated on?
Are you the other woman?
Are you cheating?

It's time to be realistic rather than idealistic.

Intimate relationships are built on compromise, self sacrifice, acceptance and an expression of appreciation for all these things.

This exercise requires you to step back from your emotional self that is driven by our need for things, like having someone pay you attention so you feel "desired" or "special". It requires you to reflect on your hurt and anger and learn how to ask questions and seek answers.

Firstly reflect on your partner's relationships with other people, not just their relationship with you. What are their **personal characteristics** you like and dislike?

Like   Dislike

_____   _____

_____   _____

_____   _____

_____   _____

_____   _____

Next, what are you really wanting from your relationship? In other words, what are your **expectations**?

_____

_____

_____

_____

_____

_____

_____

_____

Have a look back over your list, which expectations are **most important** to you?   Put a mark along side these.

Are these **reasonable** expectations of your partner? _____

Is your partner **capable** of meeting the expectations that are most important to you? _____

Is your partner **aware** of your expectations? _____

If the answer is 'no', you need to communicate honestly and calmly with your partner using assertive language such as

"I notice when you _____, I feel _____ and _____, I would prefer/ like/ want you to _____."

Which expectations are the **deal breakers** and which ones can you compromise on?

Deal Breakers   Compromise

_____   _____

_____   _____

_____   _____

_____   _____

Does your partner know what the deal breakers are, or do you expect them to just know? _____

Here are some further questions that will help you come to the right decision for your situation.

What is the 'glue' of your relationship? In other words, what are your relationship **strengths**? What is currently holding your relationship together?

_____

_____

_____

_____

What is your **vision** of your future and your lives together?

_____

_____

_____

Is it a **shared vision** with your partner? _____

What are your important **values**? (eg. motivated, kind, affectionate, determined, comfort, passion)

_____

_____

_____

Does your partner share these? _____

How do you **resolve** problems and communicate?

_____

_____

How can you change this? (if you feel you need to)

_____

What about your **shared interests**? How do you spend time together?

_____

_____

_____

How much **time** do you spend together each day or each week?

_____

Ask your partner to do this exercise and list their expectations. Are your expectations similar to your partner's?
_____

If after negotiating expectations with your partner, you find that you actually want or expect quite different things from your relationship then it's time to use your "wise self" or "inner wisdom" to consider the most appropriate actions. These decisions should not harm the person you want to be (your values and self respect).

Remember, whenever we agree to a relationship we each carry some responsibility for its success or failure.

Hopefully your decision is clearer. Listen to your gut. What is your intuition telling you? Stay or Go? _____

Write down the good and the bad things about this decision.

GOOD   NOT SO GOOD

_____   _____

_____   _____

_____   _____

_____   _____

_____   _____

_____   _____

_____   _____

_____   _____

_____   _____

_____   _____

_____   _____

LIFE BALANCE

Let's have a quick look at how you are spending your time. Below are two charts. The first one shows areas of your life, the second areas of your relationship. From a scale of 1-10 colour in the area that represents how much of your time you spend doing that section. For example: Your family. If you spend 50% of your time attending to your family, then colour (from the centre) out five sections. Complete the entire chart and reflect on where your time and energy is being spent. Now you can look at those areas that are over or under where you would like them to be so you find more balance in your life.

Areas of your Life:

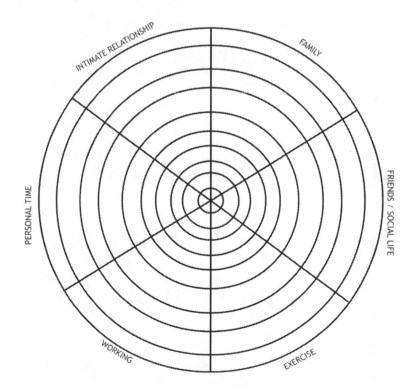

Areas within your Relationship:

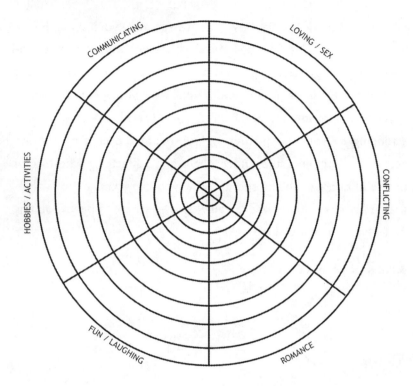

I hope this helps you find all that you are looking for in your life.

Songs and Poems that helped me along my Triangle Journeys.

When I hear this song it reminds me of Dan and the knowledge that it was over - final curtain fall, over!

FADE TO BLUE
Leann Rimes - Blue

I think I know the story's going to end,
it's getting to the part, I hate,
where heart ache closes in,
the stage is set,
it's time for me to leave,
coz I don't want to see the final scene
Fades to blue,
we didn't make it through.
Let the curtain fall and fade to blue.

We played the part of lovers,
knew each line by heart,
but sometimes Love cannot erase what's written in the stars,
so before the bitter words come crashing down,
let's leave what's left and let the lights go down.
Fades to blue, we didn't make it through.
there won't be a curtain call just fade to blue.

Almost happy endings have no way of coming true,
but the feeling starts to fade,
Fades to blue, we didn't make it through.
So let the curtain fall and fade to blue.

This is one that certainly helped me through my infidelity. I kept playing it really loud. I'll Try!

I'll TRY (to be true to you)
Alan Jackson - Greatest Hits Collection

Here we are, Talking about forever,
Both know damn well
It's not easy together,
we've both felt love, we've both felt pain,
I talk the sunshine, over the rain,
and I'll try to love only You,
and I'll try my best to be true,
oh darling, I'll try.

I'm not scared, it's worth a chance to me
Take my hand, let's face eternity
Well, I can't tell you that I'll never change
but I can swear that in every way
I'll try to love only You,
and I'll try my best to be true,
oh darling, I'll try.

I'm not perfect, just another (wo)man,
But I will give you all that I am,
and I'll try, to love only You,
and I'll try my best to be true,
oh darling, I'll try.

This is a song that I recorded and shared with Nick many, many times. I think it sumed up his situation exactly. Poor guy had to listen it often.

REASON ENOUGH
Shanley Del - What's a Heartache For?

*Lately your talking without really speaking
And lately you won't met my eyes
You come home too late without saying hello
And you leave without saying goodbye
You don't have to put into words
My heart is already hurt*

*Sometimes it just goes by
You don't really know why
You wake up and fall out of love*
**If you're thinking of leaving and needing a reason
I'd say that's reason enough**

*I know you have been wondering
What I have been feeling
But the truth is that I've felt the same
Just spinning my wheels and going no where
And looking for something to blame
I've given up just like you
There's only so much we can do*

Chorus

*Hope that you're happy whatever you do
I know that I'll make it alright
I'll come back to me, You'll go back to you
And we'll end without needing to fight
We've come to the end of the line
There's just one more lesson in life*

*Sometimes it just goes by
You don't really know why
You wake up and fall out of love*
**If you're thinking of leaving and needing a reason
I'd say that's reason enough**

This is Sean's favourite - He know's he loves me!

DON'T KNOW MUCH
Linda Ronstadt & Aaron Neville

Look at this face
I know the years are showing
Look at this life
I still don't know where it's going
I don't know much
But I know I love you
Let me be all I need to know

Look at these eyes
They never seem to matter
Look at these dreams
So big and so "believe"
I don't know much
But I know I love you
Let me be all I need to know

So many questions
Still left unanswered
So much I've never broken through
And when I feel _____
Sometimes I see so clearly
The only trouble
I've ever known
With you

Look at this man
So blessed with inspiration
Look at this soul
Still searching for salvation

I don't know much
But I know I love you
Let me be all I need to know
I don't know much
But I know I love you
Let me be all there is to know

165

This is the poem for special people that come into our lives (Aiden).

Reason, Season and Lifetime

People always come into your life for a reason, a season, or a lifetime.
When you figure out which it is, you know exactly what to do...

When someone is in your life for a REASON,
it is usually to meet a need you have expressed outwardly or inwardly.
They have come to assist you through a difficulty,
or to provide you with guidance and support,
to aid you physically, emotionally, or even spiritually.
They may seem like a godsend to you and they are.
They are there for the reason you need them to be.

Then, without any wrong doing on your part or at an inconvenient time,
this person will say or do something to bring the relationship to an end.

Sometimes they die. Sometimes they just walk away.
Sometimes they act up or out and force you to take a stand.
What we must realize is that our need has been met,
our desire fulfilled; their work is done.
The prayer you sent up has been answered and it is now time to move on.

When people come into your life for a SEASON,
it is because your turn has come to share, grow, or learn.
They may bring you an experience of peace or make you laugh.
They may teach you something you have never done.
They usually give you an unbelievable amount of joy.
Believe it! It is real! But, only for a season.
And like Spring turns to Summer and Summer to Fall,
the season eventually ends.

LIFETIME relationships teach you lifetime lessons;
those things you must build upon in order to have a solid emotional foundation.
Your job is to accept the lesson, love the person/people (anyway);
and put what you have learnt to use in all other relationships and areas in your life.
It is said that love is blind but friendship is clairvoyant.

- Unknown Author

My Thoughts / Diary Entries :   Date : ___/___/___

Today I'm Grateful for :

_____

_____

_____

_____

_____

_____

_____

_____

_____

_____

_____

_____

_____

My Thoughts / Diary Entries :   Date : ___ / ___ / ___

_____

_____

_____

_____

_____

_____

_____

_____

_____

_____

_____

_____

_____

_____

_____

Today I'm Grateful for :

_____

_____

_____

_____

_____

_____

_____

_____

_____

_____

_____

_____

_____

My Thoughts / Diary Entries :   Date : ___/___/___

_____

_____

_____

_____

_____

_____

_____

_____

_____

_____

_____

_____

_____

_____

Today I'm Grateful for :

_____

_____

_____

_____

_____

_____

_____

_____

_____

_____

_____

_____

_____

My Thoughts / Diary Entries :   Date : ___/___/___

_____

_____

_____

_____

_____

_____

_____

_____

_____

_____

_____

_____

_____

_____

Today I'm Grateful for :

My Thoughts / Diary Entries :   Date : ___/___/___

Today I'm Grateful for :

_____

_____

_____

_____

_____

_____

_____

_____

_____

_____

_____

_____

_____

My Thoughts / Diary Entries :   Date : ___/___/___

_____

_____

_____

_____

_____

_____

_____

_____

_____

_____

_____

_____

_____

_____

Today I'm Grateful for :

_____

_____

_____

_____

_____

_____

_____

_____

_____

_____

_____

_____

_____

My Thoughts / Diary Entries :   Date : ___/___/___

_____

_____

_____

_____

_____

_____

_____

_____

_____

_____

_____

_____

_____

Today I'm Grateful for :

_____

_____

_____

_____

_____

_____

_____

_____

_____

_____

_____

_____

_____

"If you would not be forgotten,
as soon as you are dead and rotten,
either write things worth reading,
or do things worth the writing."

Benjamin Franklin